THE
PROFESSOR'S
WIFE

A NOVELLA

MARINA DELVECCHIO

Black Rose Writing | Texas

ISBN: 978-1-68433-781-1
PUBLISHED BY BLACK ROSE WRITING
www.blackrosewriting.com

Printed in the United States of America
Suggested Retail Price (SRP) $15.95

The Professor's Wife is printed in Sabon

*As a planet-friendly publisher, Black Rose Writing does its best to eliminate unnecessary waste to reduce paper usage and energy costs, while never compromising the reading experience. As a result, the final word count vs. page count may not meet common expectations.

For Joseph and Marina
I live and breathe and write for you, my two hearts, my two loves.

THE
PROFESSOR'S
WIFE

CHAPTER 1

Carl Bingham's hands shook as he twisted the key to lock the main door of his home. The freckles on his fingers danced with the exertion it took him to remove the key from the lock and place it into his jacket pocket. He balanced himself by grasping the white railing and tracing its outline, slowly pacing along the wraparound porch of his farmhouse. He was thinking about the seven steps he would have to face in a few seconds leading from the top of the porch to the bottom and placing him on the gravel walkway he needed to land on to get to the pharmacist's in town.

When he reached the top of the porch landing, he hesitated a bit, to take a breath, yes, but also to marvel at the teal blue steps his wife had painted with her own hands so many years ago—before she had gotten ill—before he had to resign from his teaching job at the college to care for her. Carl was still tending to her, but worry creased his brows at the thought. He couldn't even lock the door without becoming spent. He didn't know how much longer he could protect her, or how she would survive if anything happened to him while descending her blue steps.

That Camilla of his had been a spirited girl, lovely and vibrant. Nothing like the shriveled, frail whisper of the woman now lying in their bed. The day she had painted the steps leading up to the porch of their home, he had been at work longer than expected. A tenured professor of British Literature at Skidmore College in Saratoga Springs, he had been missing a lot of dinners with his young wife. At twenty-seven, she had the wisdom and intelligence of his fifty-six years, but she was not the kind of woman one placed into a home and bid her to clean and cook and make babies. So, when her dinners remained uneaten and cold upon their dining room table, and he trudged in after nine in the evening up to his elbows in ungraded student papers, her patience had worn thin.

"You leave me in this big old house by myself all day and then you return to me late. It's been three nights this week," she whined.

"Honey," he began, beckoning her to sit next to him on the couch, where he had propped his feet upon the coffee table. Camilla pouted as she slowly made her way to him and then sat upon his lap, facing him, and flattening the lapels of his tweed jacket to his shoulder blades. Her touch still made him shiver, and they had been married three years. They made love almost every night, and she was no stranger to the things he liked.

"You're supposed to be painting, anyway," he sighed, closing his eyes so he could feel her fingers touching his neck and face from a dark and disembodied place that always felt so good. "Did you get to paint a bit?"

"I sure did," Camilla piped up, rose from his lap suddenly, and then pulled him off the couch. "Let me show you."

Carl thought she would drag him up the stairs to their bedroom, to continue the journey her fingers had begun from his neck to his hair and then back down again to his collarbone and the trail of grey wiry chest strands she had unbuttoned his shirt to get to. Instead, she pulled him to the front door, yanked it open, and led him to the center of their wrap-around porch, which curved over them like a bell at the top of the seven steps.

"Look," she pointed to the seven steps that stretched out beneath them.

His eyes followed the path of her fingers, but he saw nothing except the steps.

"Oh, Carl!" Camilla left him standing there, disappeared into the house, and turned on the porch light from inside. "You see anything different now?"

"Indeed, I do," he chuckled. She had painted the stairs teal blue. "Very nice."

"Well, I got tired of waiting for you, so I whipped out the paint that we used for our bedroom walls, and voila! The exterior of the house is all white, and I just couldn't stand it anymore. It's so blah. So, I painted it blue, like our bedroom. Maybe the steps will remind you of our bed and the sex that awaits you, and you will come home to me instead of playing around with your little wide-eyed undergraduates."

"Indeed, I will," he grinned, planting a kiss on her dark hair and pulling her close to him. "Indeed, I will."

Carl smiled, thinking of his wife, when she was young and feisty. He still saw that girl in the woman who lay in their bed upstairs; he saw that girl in her eyes when she smiled as he offered her medicine to dull her pain. But mostly he saw her pain. Pain he couldn't take away. It's not like it used to be, when she hurt inside and cried on his shoulders, and he could take it all away with just one cajoling comment or a quote from Keats or Byron. That always made her mood lift a bit, and then she would brighten up, kiss him on the lips, and go about her business, renovating a kitchen cabinet, or sanding down a table, or painting the guest bedroom a different color.

That was a different Camilla, a long time ago Camilla. One that ran across their lawn in her tank top and shorts or bustled into the kitchen with a new meal she had found on the internet, pounding away at the keyboard applying for grants to study with a particular artist, or shimmying out of her clothes and climbing into bed with him, covering the expanse of his chest with her dark strands, her lips moist upon his skin.

Carl hesitated at the base of the blue teal steps, grabbed onto the railing, and looked upward at the window above him. Their bedroom window. Where she lay, groaning in pain, writhing in discomfort. He could still hear the soft moans that forced their way out of her lips, lips that once grinned with mischief. Lips that found his again and again with a hunger he envied in her, a hunger he could not satisfy no matter how often he made love to her, how much food he fed her, how many talents she picked up and dropped back down when they got too heavy for her to carry. She lay in that bed of theirs, and after decades of marriage and love and passion, she was still empty. He felt the yawning hunger inside her even now—while he stood outside their home, on his way to the pharmacy for her medicine. Not even the medicine could fill her appetite or the emptiness that took up most of her, growing, duplicating, stretching as far as her insides would allow. She was full of drugs, but she was empty.

Her eyes told him every day—the soft earthy shade of dust and soil looking back at him with pain, pleading with him for something he couldn't quite put his finger on. Desire. No, he felt the desire. He was sure she desired nothing now. Except release. She wanted release from this earth, this world that failed her again and again. And from him, too. Because even after all these years, he did not know the trick to loving her so she felt it. And this, he was sure, is how he had failed her.

CHAPTER 2

Camilla sat in the back of the lecture hall in Dr. Bingham's British Literature course, trying hard not to yawn. She thought little of the older man who rattled off poetic lines from Keats and Byron; he was older, in his late fifties. He wasn't handsome, not in the way she liked the young men she played with to be handsome, with chiseled features and a tough exterior. She liked broad shoulders and large hands—large enough to disappear into when they touched her beneath her shirt. And when they climbed on top of her, she liked to disappear then, too, beneath their strength and their rippling muscles. There was something beautiful about being overcome by large men.

Camilla was tall herself, 5'11, so she liked her lovers to be taller, wider, stronger. She wanted to feel small beside them, in body at least. Enjoyed when they took control and seemed to know exactly what she wanted without her ever telling them. Those were the men she desired, men her body responded to without her even thinking about it. She usually complied with her body's urges. Her body followed her to school and work and conspired with her to get what she deemed important, and she reciprocated by following her body's inclinations for men who could satisfy the needs she didn't quite understand herself.

Sometimes she felt like an animal that needed feeding, and these beasts were the only ones who could feed her. And they did, for a while, as long as they remained inside her or on top of her. But as soon as they left, or moved away, she felt the absence of their warmth, their strength, the echo of their fingers on her skin, and she was dull again. She filled the vast emptiness with guy after guy, but nothing stuck, and she was never sure why or how she had ended up like this, hungry all the time, unoccupied all the time.

She tried to feed herself in other ways. Tried relationships, hobbies, books, traveling, but nothing. The only time she felt good, full, was when she was having sex, and even that left a gaping hole in her afterwards. At twenty-seven, she realized she didn't have the tools to figure herself out.

Bringing her pen into her mouth out of frustration, she released a long sigh, pushed her head back against her lecture chair, and closed her eyes. She tried to shut every thought and irritation out of her mind. Everything except his voice. Dr. Bingham, she realized, had a lovely sound to him. His tone was gentle, and there was a cadence to his lecture, as if he were speaking directly to her, calming her, talking her out of her angst.

Her body responded to his voice, relaxing under the soothing flow of his words, and even her heart beat to the rhythm of his speech patterns—tu-tum, tu-tum, tu-tum. His voice was a caress, and she felt the tension in her limbs loosen and untie.

Camilla shook her head and opened her eyes to inspect this strange man again. Sitting up, she dragged her weary eyes to his only to find his hazel ones staring right at her. They were large and bright, and they were pinned on her. She felt the force of them on her face, and she blushed. She never blushed. It's as if he could see right through her, into her, and this ability to see her felt more powerful than when men lay on top of her, their hands pushing her down, their hips rolling onto hers.

Her heart pulsed loudly in her ears. Camilla was paralyzed for the moment, staring back at a man she had not seen before even though she had been in his course for the past six weeks. A man unlike the ones she had known and seen naked—an older man, whose tired, aging eyes looked back at her with humor.

The moment one feels seen by another human being is transformative. You feel awakened for the first time; at least, that's how it was for Camilla. She felt the flush of chills cascade through her blood and find root in the marrow of her bones. The hairs on her arms and legs stood up, as if they were reaching for the one person who had stirred life into them.

Camilla was awake. For the first time in her life, she felt fixed and in control. Her feet touched the earth beneath her, and she tasted satisfaction in her mouth. Her stomach settled, and as she walked out of the classroom, her legs guided her to his office. She almost ran to him.

"Professor Bingham?" She queried, knocking on the splintered oak door that was slightly ajar.

"Come in," he beckoned. He was sitting behind an old desk, surrounded by papers he needed to grade. His bifocals rested low on his nose, revealing the slight hooked bone that protruded, giving him an austere and chiseled look. He appeared younger to her close up. He was definitely in his late fifties. She had the urge to take his glasses off, breathe on them, and clean them with the edges of her sweater. She could see specks of dust on them all the way from the worn leather couch she was now sitting in, dropping her book bag on the beige, coffee-stained carpet that covered the floor of his small office.

She pulled her eyes away from him, and the act itself took her breath away. It was as if she was leaving home. She shuddered as an icy chill crept up to her scalp and closed her eyes for a second. When she opened them again, she found him looking at her, his eyes gently resting on her features.

"What can I help you with?" His voice pulled her out of the fog of her thoughts, and she thought she saw him reaching out for her, his hands grabbing hold of hers and pulling her out of a cavernous hole of nothingness. That is where she had been suspended for most of her life, looking out at the world as if she didn't quite belong to it. And here he was, pulling her back into it, without even a word.

"Camilla Jones, right?" He prodded.

She didn't answer him. She didn't think she needed to. He knew why she was there. She saw it in his eyes, in the smile that played with the freckles on his face. They both knew what was happening between them even while seated opposite one another with a large, paper-saddled oak desk and over twenty-five years of difference between them.

She turned around in her seat to capture the contents of his office. He had two bookcases, all double-decked with books on poets and novels, both contemporary and the classics, in alphabetical order. Because there was no more space on the bookcases, it seems he had begun piling the books on the floor; right now, he had four separate piles situated around his desk, like armor. And she saw this in him. Books were his protection from the outside world. He lived in his office and in his work, in the writing of his poets and his students. There was nothing more for him. No wedding ring on his finger, no lover on the side. He had retired from all pleasures outside of books and teaching. But she also saw that he was content; when he smiled, it was genuine, taking pleasure in seeing things that no one else saw.

"You saw me." Camilla's whisper broke through the warm blanket shrouding them.

"Yes," he smiled at her again. "You were napping during my lecture."

"No." Camilla shook her head.

"No?" His smile wavered, and she could see his bottom lip quiver slightly, emitting a light inside her. She could feel its heat. She could feel it expanding and pushing away all the darkness living there.

She inched forward in her seat, placed her palms on the edges of his desk, and took hold of his light eyes with her dark ones.

"You see me."

She heard the huskiness in her own voice, the firm way it cornered him in his chair and would not let him escape her meaning.

"Yes." He whispered back. "I see you."

With that, she rose from her chair and closed the distance between them. Standing above him, she leaned forward, cupped his face with the palm of her hands, and touched her lips to his. He tasted like coffee, and she deepened the kiss, trying to reach him where he hid. When she sensed him surrender, she moved one hand to his chest so she could feel his heart beating against her, and it wasn't until his hand rested on her hip and his tongue responded to her calling that their kiss mimicked the rhythm of his blood pumping with wild abandon against her hand.

"I can't," Carl whispered against her mouth after a long moment. "I'm sorry, I can't do this." He pried his fingers from her hips and put his hand in the air between them, as if surrendering at gunpoint.

"You can't, what?" She asked coyly, running her tongue over her lips, tasting the coffee remnants that lived in his mouth, on his tongue as it swirled around hers. Like a snake, slippery and knowing. Camilla surmised he would be a wonderful lover, and the thought of him on top of her sent chills up her spine, causing her to shiver slightly in her shoes. She circled around the other side of his desk and took her place opposite him, in the student chair, the brown leather giving in to her slight weight.

"I never should have kissed you." The words rushed out of his mouth in spurts, winded by the excursion. Her smile widened at the thrill of the power she obviously had on him. Camilla wanted more.

"Well, I kissed you," she corrected. "Although you did kiss me back." Camilla enjoyed teasing him, watching him shift in his chair, trying to figure out what to do with his fingers on the desk. He took some loose, ungraded papers and stacked them on top of each other. Then he put them in front of him. Finally, he picked them up again and moved them to the right. He straightened his phone cord. Wiped a bit of dust off the screen with this thumb, hoping, she guessed, that someone would pick this time to call him. To interrupt their interlude. She found him endearing. And that kiss. That kiss made her feel all the feels that she had not encountered before with any guy. It's as if he was reciting poetry in her mouth, seducing her with song and lyricism. He enthralled her, and she decided right there that she wouldn't leave his office until he consented to a date. Just a date. What could possibly happen? Her thighs burned with anticipation.

"I'm your professor. There are rules. I can't have relationships with my students." He sat back in his chair and tried hard not to look at her. She stared at him until his eyes met hers. She smiled with approval.

"Do people still follow this rule? It's so antiquated." Camilla yawned to show that this line of discourse bored her. That rules bored her. She pulled out her phone from her back-jean pocket and started tapping on the screen.

"What are you doing?" Carl was frustrated with this girl, half afraid of losing his tenured position at the college and half afraid of what she would do next.

"Just give me a minute, Professor." Looking down at her screen, her fingers adeptly moving over its surface, she deepened her smile.

"OK," she said after a while. "We're free."

"What do you mean, we're free?"

"I just dropped your course. I'm no longer your student, your insubordinate, and you are no longer my superior. We're equals now. Just Carl and Camilla."

Carl was dumbfounded. He sank back into his chair as if someone pushed the wind out of him. "You dropped my course? Why?"

"Because I want to date you, silly. Don't you want to date me?"

Camilla placed her elbows on the edge of his desk, noting the dust circles collected on the surface, and decided that once they became lovers, she would come back and clean this room up. Remove the dust and the clutter that breathed like gray clouds all around him, rendering him almost invisible. Almost. She saw him. And she liked what she saw. The gray orbs of his eyes that flashed with desire when she kissed him. The way his chest hair, white and wiry, crowded the frame of his chest and forced their way out from the unbuttoned top of his white shirt. The tidy manner with which he cuffed the shirt sleeves up his arms, showing the strength of his muscles when he moved. Feeling that strength when he circled the same arms around her waist and pulled her closer into him. The way his body vibrated against hers like the low vibrato sounds that grew out of a bass instrument, its thick strings strummed with just one's fingertips. Low, deep, and sonorous. She was lulled by him, and in his arms, she was found. Yes, she fit into him perfectly, and she wouldn't pass him by the way all the other girls had, seeing just an old man who had exhausted all his chances at love.

"Well?" She probed, leaning her chest against the edge of his desk, knowing full well her low fitted shirt exposed the mounds of her breasts, puckering at him. She saw his eyes struggle to focus on her and not on the flesh that she pushed and ground against the wooden furniture. When his eyes met hers again, that flash of desire was there, the one she captured right before her mouth claimed his. Oh, how she wanted to taste him again. To know the feel of him inside her for the first time. She imagined loving him would be different from all the men she'd been with. Maybe more careful with her, more cautious, maybe even more loving.

"There's some history with me, you know. Some unpleasant history." His voice was low, husky, out of breath, as if he had just run a marathon and hadn't quite recovered. Camilla took this as a good sign. He hadn't kicked her out of his office, so there was still hope.

"You mean the rumor about the girl that died? Yeah, I heard about it. The girls around here talk about everyone, and you're a mystery to them. But it's just that. A rumor, right?"

"No. It's not a rumor. I almost lost my job, my tenure. It was a long time ago. When I was younger and more foolish, but I haven't consorted with young women in my courses since. I don't plan on it again."

"But you've consorted with young women on campus?" She queried, her tone flirtatious and feminine. Inviting, even.

"No. No women from campus. Not even my colleagues. I almost lost everything that was important to me, including my self-respect. So that's not a road I endeavor to go down ever again." He sat up in his chair, armed with poise and confidence.

Camilla nodded her head with thoughtful understanding, afraid to lose him to rules and regulations and fears.

"Tell me about it. About her. Let me at least have a choice in the matter. Or better yet, tell me so I can put those rumors to bed."

The sigh he released was so heavy and long, it seemed to take forever for his body to expel it.

"I don't know you," he began. "And I'm a private person." Carl's voice was tremulous as the words made their way out of him. He pressed his fingers beneath his thighs so their trembling wouldn't reveal him to this beauty that sat before him, smiling still, a knowing look in her eyes that kept him prisoner in his office, in his seat, his eyes locked with hers in a battle of secret wants and longings he hadn't let himself consider in so many years.

"You know me, Professor. You just had your arms around me, your tongue in my mouth. Let's not play any more games. You know where this is going."

He closed his eyes and readied himself to reveal the parts of him he had buried so long ago. He didn't know how much he wanted this, this intimacy, this awakening until she kissed him. It's as if her kiss, the touch of her hands on his chest, his chin, her eyes in his, had woken him up, reminding him of what it felt like to be wanted, desired even. Or to be touched. How long had it been since he'd known the touch of a woman? Not since Isabella.

"I fell in love with one of my students." He gave birth to the secrets of his past, releasing them into the musty air of his office. But the girl who sat before him, her eyes wide and calm, took it all in, without flinching, without judging. He continued. "I was twenty-eight, had just gotten my Ph.D., and Skidmore was the first college to offer me a position. I had everything I had worked so hard to attain. And then this girl came into my life. Isabella. Even her name was like poetry. She was young, innocent, quiet. Lovely, too. She kept coming to my office, all the time. Isabella bumped into me at coffee shops in the area, in the parking lots on campus. She was everywhere. And each time, we had these long conversations that went on for hours just to continue the next time I bumped into her. It happened so often that eventually, I welcomed her visits, her sudden appearances, and if I didn't see her, there was an ache in me, like I lost something precious. One day, I kissed her. It felt right, like I was meant to kiss her, love her."

Carl paused to look at Camilla.

"You remind me a bit of her, you know."

"I do?" She smiled, taking this concession as a positive move in the direction she wanted him to follow. A direction that would lead him back to her.

He nodded, a faint smile slipping along his lips and loosening the tightness around his mouth. "She had dark hair, almost black, and her eyes. I could look into them for hours, uncovering worlds belying her small and quiet demeanor. She had such depth. We talked about poetry and some of her favorite writers: Grimke, Dickinson, Browning, Rossetti. All women. Strong, virile, brilliant women. She was a poet, too."

Camilla nodded, reminding herself to be patient as he told the story that she needed to unhook from his denials and fears in order to get to him. To make him hers.

"We tried to be discreet, but rumors made their way to administration. They told me to end the relationship or find another job. I chose my career. I loved her, but I suppose I loved my career more. It seems like a senseless choice to me now, but I was young, the entire world still laid out before me. I broke up with her, and the next thing I know, she killed herself. Her roommate found her in the tub, her wrists sliced, her body naked and blood-soaked. The college put me on paid leave for a year, until the rumors died down, and then let me resume my role at the college. I had to sign an agreement that I would not pursue any relationships with women at the college. So you see, I cannot... what's the term you used? Date you. I just can't."

"That wasn't your fault, Carl. You shouldn't blame yourself over her death."

"Whose fault was it then?" Camilla wanted to reach over and wipe the frown off his face. It made him look dull and old. And he was so much more than that.

"She killed herself. She was the weak one. And this thing you signed; it's not binding. No one can tell you who to love or who to date."

"She was just a kid. I should've known better."

"You couldn't have expected that outcome, that she would take her own life. Just because you broke up with her. Listen, if you break up with me, I guarantee you, I won't try to kill myself. Women are made of different stuff nowadays. We're stronger. Worldly. We don't kill ourselves over men. Or professors. No matter how good-looking and sexy they are."

Camilla waited for her last words to sink into him, and when they did, his gaze was dark and full of wanting.

"I'm not Isabella and you're not the young, naïve man you were with her. I'm not a child, and I know what I want."

"I can't," he whispered thickly, but she could hear the resignation in his voice.

She waited until the desire she found in his eyes when she kissed him earlier resurfaced. It was in the flecks of his eyes when he looked at her, the way they rested on her face, without reservation. It was as if he was surrendering to her, letting her decide for him.

"Take me out," she instructed him, sitting back in the leather chair, confident of his response. "I want to see you as a man and have you see me as a woman. Because that's all that we are. And I want you. You want me, too. I can see it." She paused. "I want you to want me."

"Yes." He swallowed, the sound a confirmation of what she confessed. "I'll take you out." They both smiled then, and she knew when she walked out the door, feeling the full weight of his eyes on her back, that he would be the last man she would ever love. He was the one.

CHAPTER 3

Camilla had lived most of her life as a ghost. Carl was the first person to see her. To see into her, past the ink-black hair and chocolate deep eyes, the cleft in her chin, and the curvy shell containing her.

"How can you sleep with him?" Her roommate, Chelsea, asked, her nose crinkled in the mirror, looking at Camilla through the reflection of the glass. "He's so old."

"He's not that old," Camilla laughed at her friend. They met in History of Art class at Skidmore. They were both working on their graduate degrees, and when Camilla's head sank into Chelsea's shoulder during one lecture because she had fallen asleep, Chelsea only smiled and let the dark-haired girl sleep on her without awakening her. When the class was over, Chelsea placed a gentle hand on Camilla's and squeezed it until she woke.

"Class is over," Chelsea's husky voice burrowed into Camilla's drowsiness, lulling her awake. "You want to get some coffee while you go over my notes?"

Camilla pulled her heavy head back into her chair and space, grateful for the small blond girl whose name she didn't even know yet.

"Yeah, sure." Camilla's voice came out hoarse and grateful. "I'm Camilla."

Chelsea laughed, and the sound was like those huge bells ringing from church towers in old cities she often saw and heard in movies, loud and gruff and vibrating throughout Camilla's body. Chelsea was small, not even 5'1, maybe 108 pounds heavy, but she occupied the spaces around her like they belonged to her.

"I'm Chelsea." She whipped out her hand, and Camilla took it, laughing at the formality. They shook hands that day, one year ago, and since then, they hadn't known a day without seeing each other's face. They ate together, studied together, and partied together, sometimes waking up with hangovers and sleeping boys in their beds, meeting in the common area of the kitchen just to giggle about how good, or bad, the sex had been.

"I love you," Camilla said to her the night they moved in together. They had just brought in the last of the boxes from their respective cars and piled them into the middle of what would be their living room. Chelsea's slight frame sank into the large red beanbag they tossed on the floor, leaving room for Camilla, who plopped down beside her. A farting sound emitted from the force of her body falling on it, and they both burst into laughter, heads bent, touching, blond waves intertwining with ink-black strands. It was then that Camilla felt this bubble of awe yawning inside her chest, pulling her ribcage apart, filling its interior with light and a sensation she had never encountered before.

"I love you, too," Chelsea sighed into Camilla's hair and took in a breath, inhaling the scent of lilacs from her shampoo and musk from her clammy skin, both familiar and sweet. Camilla reached out for Chelsea's fingers and held them in her palm, running her fingers over the silver rings on her thumb and forefinger. "You're my blood sister, Camilla. My tribe. Never forget that."

"I've never been part of a tribe," Camilla confessed to her friend. "What's that like?"

"Well," Chelsea began, shifting her body so that she could look into her friend's eyes. "It's better than family. We don't choose our family, you know. We're born into it. I didn't choose my drunken father or my weak mother. I didn't choose the fact that he snuck into my room in the middle of the night to touch me under my clothes between the ages of seven and fifteen and then sit across from me at breakfast, pretending it hadn't happened. Family is dysfunctional and full of defective people who won't stand up for you. At least, that's how mine was. Tribe is the family you choose. The people you choose to be with, who support you and who will sacrifice for you. You're my tribe, Camilla. Whatever you need. Whenever you need it."

Camilla laughed. "That's the best proposal I've ever received. Sometimes, you make me wish I was gay. You're like the best boyfriend I've ever had."

"Oh, yeah. If I were into chicks, you'd be it for me. Unfortunately for both of us, we're into guys, but let me tell you, the pickings are slim. Is it me, or do they seem to be getting worse? It's like all the good ones have been picked up and married off already."

"Yeah. At our age, it's like we're stuck with the rowdy drunk ones. But I'm not looking for marriage. I don't think I'll ever marry."

"You say that now, Camilla. But who knows what will happen in the future? You may find someone and change your mind."

"I doubt it. I can't seem to connect with anyone other than for one night. In the morning, I just want them to get the fuck out of my bed, and I can't even look at them."

"You connected with me," Chelsea reminded her, nudging her in the shoulder with a slight twist of her own body.

"You're different. You're you. Easy and open, with a heart that is big and loud. I can't ignore it."

"Yeah, but it also means that you can connect. There's nothing wrong with you. You just need the right guy to connect with. You'll see. It'll happen."

Chelsea was right, because a year later, Camilla connected with someone. He wasn't young or cool and he didn't hang out at bars, but Carl gripped her with his voice, his eyes, pulling her into him without even saying a word. That was the connection she was yearning for and found in the most uncommon of places and men.

She knew Chelsea didn't like Carl. There was something off about him, Chelsea told her. She had taken a course with him last semester, and there was something cold and off-putting in his eyes, Chelsea warned her. But Camilla knew this was just her tribe-leader being insecure about her friend finding solace in another person, a man this time. A man with a home and a career and the maturity of an adult, not the young guys they met in clubs or bars and brought home for one-night flings. This had been their ritual since they met. They had done everything together, and now Camilla was spending most of her time away from their apartment and their usual bar scenes. Even when they hung out, it was different since Chelsea would bring home a guy, and Camilla did not, often leaving the bar as soon as Chelsea showed signs of hooking up.

"Look, I know he's older than the guys we date, and I know you get the creeps from him. But I'm telling you. Something in him recognized me and something in me recognized him." She sat next to Chelsea as she fixed her hair to go out on a date with some guy from her sketching course. "I need you to trust me. To support me. He's different, but in a good way."

Chelsea applied the last of her dark brown lipstick on her lips, puckered them at her reflection in the mirror, and turned in her chair to face Camilla. "We're family, remember? I can tell you I don't like the guy, but I still love and support you. I'm just going to look out for you, too. It's my job."

Camilla smiled. "I love you."

"And I love you. Always." Chelsea kissed Camilla on the forehead and rose. "I have to meet up with Matt. You sure you don't want to go with us? We're just meeting for drinks at the pub down the block."

"No, thanks. Carl's cooking for me. At his place."

"Should I expect to see you later?" Chelsea winked at her.

"I don't think so. I think tonight is the night." Camilla smiled, thinking of falling asleep in Carl's arms for the first time.

"I'll see you later, then. Love you."

"Yeah. Later. Love you, too." Camilla's response was absent-minded, her eyes fixed on the clothes stretched out in her closet, so she didn't even notice Chelsea exiting their apartment. She was already thinking about what to wear, her skin itching with the want of being touched again by her professor.

CHAPTER 4

Camilla drove her white Acura Integra along the winding dirt road leading to the oldest and grandest Victorian house she had ever seen. It was white, its paint chipped and cracked from age and neglect, with equally dull and drooping shutters adorning each side of all the windows. There were three floors that she could determine and a wraparound porch with a wooden swing hanging from its roof. She didn't need to see the interior of the house to love it. She slowed down her car, dust billowing about her side windows and mirrors, and the only vision she could secure was the house and the way it leaned a bit to the side, as if it were growing old and weak and couldn't hold itself straight anymore. It reminded her of Carl Bingham. It seemed exactly like the house he would live in, sleep in, moving from room to room and occupying each open space with love and a knowing she recognized in him.

Parking her car in front of the garage, she got out and climbed the seven steps leading to the base of the veranda. Camilla sat on the swing, half-afraid it would split and crumble beneath her slight weight, leaned her head back against the wooden seat, and pushed her feet off the floor. Her body and the swing were one, swaying in unison with the music she heard coming from inside the house, a sweet, haunting melody she didn't recognize. She closed her eyes to inhabit the song sounds of crickets and frogs and the combined smells of roasted chicken and freshly cut grass. She was home.

"Are you going to stand there and watch me the entire time?" She felt his presence without seeing him, and the notion of him watching her, taking her in, quickened her pulse, the muscles in her stomach tightening with want.

He chuckled then, a low vibrating sound, the hum of a guitar string being plucked. It glided along the hairs of her arms until it found root. Throbbing from within.

"Would you like a drink, Camilla? A glass of wine, perhaps?"

"Do you have lemonade?" She asked as if startled, her eyes opening wide and scanning the doorway until they found him standing behind the screen, in the shadows. "Sitting here, on this swing, surrounded by grass and open sky, it feels like I should have lemonade right about now. Something refreshing."

"Of course. I'll be right back." She saw his shadow retreating and felt a coolness touch her skin, as if he had taken warmth away from her.

Camilla rose from her seat and followed him into the house. There was an open office space with a desk full of papers to her left, a long corridor that led to the kitchen, and a staircase leading to the upstairs rooms on the right-hand side of the house. She steered towards the path he had taken, seeking him out in the back of the house where she assumed the kitchen would be. He had disappeared from her sight, but she pursued the scents of chicken and lemon and spices the likes of oregano and pepper and paprika. She found him pouring lemonade from a wide pitcher into a tall glass sprinkled with ice. She took a seat on the other side of the blue-gray marble island. His long, lanky body was steeped in steam and the scent of herbs, making her stomach flutter with hunger. Or maybe it was him, the way he turned around to face her, the island still between them. The way he held onto the glass and pushed it toward her. The way she took hold of the glass, her fingers slowly glossing over his, the feel of his rounded knuckles soft with hair that rose to meet her touch.

"Thanks," she whispered, her voice catching on desire the way a cracked toenail latches on to a single thread on a blanket, with some resistance and a second of pain. A bittersweet sort of pain, an aching that lived inside her bones. The kind she was not aware of until it sprang up on her, like sharp needles searing into her skin when she wasn't looking.

She took a sip of the lemonade, tossed him a careless smile, and retraced her steps back to the swing where she was sure he would follow. A few moments later, he found his place beside her, and she let her head fall onto his shoulders, the cool lemonade glass pressed against her neck and collarbone for the extra cooling she needed, the night's breeze scattering goose bumps against her skin like a million bright stars twinkling against the darkening sky above them.

"Take me to bed, Professor," she whispered into his neck.

"Yes." His voice was a husky breath that overtook her. She was heady and heavy leaning into him, and when his arms wrapped around her and pulled her to his chest, she felt him rise and carry her with him through the door, up the stairs, and into his bedroom as if it had all been a dream.

And now, lying in the middle of his bed, a large king-sized panel bed made of thick oak, she wanted to be overwhelmed by him, to let him take charge. She lay there drunk on nothing more than lemonade and desire, a pretend-virgin aware of his smooth hands taking off her shoes and skirt and shirt, leaving behind only her briefs and bra. She placed her fingers on her breasts, beneath the fabric of her bra, and smiled as he took off his own clothes, brown corduroy slacks, white buttoned-down shirt, and gray boxer shorts.

He stood at the foot of the bed, naked and beautiful, his eyes breathing in the rhythmic heaving of her chest, her hands reaching out to him, inviting him to come to her, to cover her, to crush her underneath his full, glorious weight. She wanted to suffocate beneath him, to struggle for air she could only find in his mouth as he exhaled his own breath into hers. And when he entered her body, it's as if she was being made love to for the first time. Like all the other sex she'd known had been foreplay between boys and girls in dark closets on a childish dare.

This is the sex she was yearning for but couldn't articulate since she started having sex at thirteen. The kind of love parents and friends and unknowing lovers had not been able to meet for her. This was the love that had remained absent from her life, absent from her body. The kind that made her disappear into herself, as if she were a ghost cascaded by light, lost in sensations of touch and ardor and the pain that comes with connecting to a human being outside of herself. Camilla was present and absent. Lost and found. She was crushed, barely able to catch her breath, gasping with the sweet agony of death and love all wrapped up in the one man whose body blended into hers until she orgasmed and screamed with exultation.

He understood her, read her the way he read deeply into his poems, dissecting one word after the other until the puzzle of images and inner meanings were laid out before him with the ease she never found in people. Camilla wept, lying beneath him still, her arms and legs coiled around his back and thighs, as if she were a snake securing her meal, keeping him inside her for as long as she could, her limbs trembling with fatigue from being both ravaged and discovered.

"Thank you," she breathed into his ear, kissed the lobe that smelled of muskiness and ear wax, and released his body from her tight hold, escaping into a deep sleep she hadn't been able to secure since she was a little girl and her father had sung her into a dream state.

CHAPTER 5

With the pharmacist's bag in his left hand, Carl gripped the railings of his wife's blue steps. Standing at the bottom, his feet surrounded by the brown and yellow foliage of autumn, Carl looked up the steps he had to climb to get into his house, and then remembered the steps he would have to climb inside the house to get to his wife. He raised his eyes to the top-floor window, wondering how she was doing. He had taken longer than expected at the pharmacy. Usually, it was a fast run, but he had to pause twice to catch his breath. He wasn't aging well, and the few mild mini strokes he'd had in the past had left their stain on him.

The idea of climbing all those stairs exhausted him, so he sat on the bottom stoop, looking away from the house and the wife waiting for him. Carl would have to move her downstairs, into his office. He didn't use it anymore, only going in there to find a book or a poem. He spent most of his days reading to Camilla, and his evenings were spent curled up beside her, burrowing into her warmth like a child.

He touched the cool surface of the blue steps and felt the thrill that had consumed Camilla when she had painted them. They had made love on these steps that first night, and many nights afterward. Before Camilla, he would never have made love outside, let alone on the steps leading into his home. He had always been so conservative, so closed. He had only wanted his books and his quiet, unperturbed life.

"Such a fool," Carl caught himself saying aloud. He looked around to see if anyone had heard him and then chuckled softly under his breath. Only the trees could hear him and the tulips that Camilla had planted and nurtured into growth.

Carl had been a fool to think life without love was worth living. He had resigned to this, never asking of the world or of himself for more than just passable living. A good job teaching, a home full of books, and solitude was all he had desired. Until Camilla, that is. After a look or a taste of her, he realized there was so much more.

It wasn't just the sex. He had lived most of his life without it. Sex for him wasn't extraordinary. It was confusing, and he hated to be out of control or confused. He had many relationships when he was younger that had revolved around sex, but sex with just anyone was not worth it to him. What was more important was what happened before and after sex. How the woman curled into the crook of his arm or turned her body toward the wall. That's how he understood the needy ones from the distant ones. Women were complicated, and they carried with them baggage that lay between them during sex, after sex, and everywhere in between. Relationships were complicated without sex, and sex just made it more awkward, more difficult. So, he had resolved to live his life without women or sex, until Camilla.

He knew it wasn't right to love her, to make love to her. She had been only twenty-seven to his fifty-six. He had been her teacher. Such relationships were frowned upon, and before her, he had been among those punished because of them. But he had no choice. He loved her the moment her eyes locked with his; she was like a siren that willed him to her, and he could not say no. He didn't want to. She filled every hole in his life, every crevice untouched by love and softness, and he would be certifiably insane to cast her out simply because of their age difference and his position as her teacher. The only authority he had over her was poetry, but she was his teacher in everything else.

She taught him to love in the ways he found in his poetry but could never master—with all of himself, naked, unrestrained, vociferously loud and wild. Camilla loosened the reins he had placed upon his body and affections, and he would be forever grateful to her for that freedom. At twenty-seven, she had more wisdom and strength than he did in one of his middle-aged thumbs. It was amazing to him how much of our lives we spend tamping down our desires for the sake of self-preservation or because it's the easiest, least scary path to take.

What's the worst that could happen? Your wife could get sick, depression growing like wild crabgrass inside her organs. You could lose all that love and the life you had been waiting for but denied yourself out of stupidity and stubbornness, believing you didn't deserve it. Yes, he was losing all of this—the happiness he had possessed for the past twenty years with Camilla—but it had all been worth the pain he was enduring now. The pain of slowly watching the succor of joy and life being sucked out of her diminutive and failing body. He was as powerless as he was the day she had kissed him in his office all those years ago, trying to muster the courage not to touch her, not to pull her body between his thighs and press her into his desire, not to grab her hair and bring her kiss deeper into his mouth.

But he didn't regret any of it. Not the pain, the affairs, the violent arguments, and not even the sickness and the dying parts. He had loved all of her, all the time, and he loved her still, without a single trace of the Camilla he had loved, save her eyes. Those dark, lovely eyes glancing back at him with all the memories they contained.

Carl pushed against the blue step he was resting on with one hand and used the right one to pull himself erect. He shuffled from step to step until he stood beneath the gazebo-style center of their porch, under which they had shared many kisses. He could count them, all those moments shared, all those kisses felt. They played back to him like a movie, seamlessly segueing from scene to scene, from kiss to kiss. Their love story was always playing itself out in his thoughts, no matter what he was doing or what he was thinking. He was full of Camilla moments, and he wanted nothing more than to live in them all the time.

He hesitated for a second, not wanting to shift out of an unfinished clip, and then moved toward the door frame of his home with a loose smile playing on his mouth.

"Honey, I'm home," he bellowed in his usual Desi Arnaz impersonation. He heard her rustling in the covers upstairs and knew she was fine. He hated to leave her all alone, but she had expressed more pain than usual, and he wanted to acquire the medicine she needed before the store closed for the day. There was no need for her to feel so much pain in her last days. He wanted to make her as comfortable as possible.

Hanging up his jacket, or what Camilla liked to call the professor's lab coat, a brown tweed herringbone jacket fashioned with elbow patches, he grabbed the Walgreens bag and made his way up the sixteen steps to get to their bedroom.

"Good morning, darling." His voice was soft, as if to cocoon her. "I have your medicine for you. You weren't lonely while I was out, were you? I tried to hurry, but Mrs. Jennison was there, and she kept asking a ton of questions about you. Maybe if you feel better later, you can call her. They probably all think I'm holding you hostage in here."

Carl walked past her as he spoke, catching sight of her as she lay on her side of their king-sized poster bed—the right side. He made his way into the master bathroom they shared and started unloading the bottles she needed to help her feel better. He returned with a glass of water and one blue pill that rested in the crumpled palm of his hand.

"Here you go, darling." He held out his hand to her, hoping she could muster enough strength today to pick up the pill and place it inside her mouth on her own, but she didn't. She just looked at him with those great big eyes—eyes that never ceased to remind him of her youth, her vitality. Eyes that still made him desire her, even in her sunken state.

"Don't worry, sweetheart. I got it." He smiled at the gratitude he saw in her expression and placed the pill into the warm crevice of her mouth. He raised the glass to her lips, braced the back of her head with his free hand, and tipped the glass until the water trickled into her mouth. Some of it oozed back out, drawing a swirling path of liquid down her pallid chin, which he wiped with the corner of her sheet.

"Sorry about that," he said, wiping away the extra drops of water that trailed along a crease down her neck, resting like beads upon the bony structure of her clavicle. "You look tired," he pointed out. "Do you want me to read to you a bit? How about some Blake this time?"

He smiled and moved closer to her, covering the loose and mangled hair atop her scalp with his hand. Her head seemed so small, fragile in his grasp, and he watched as his thumb caressed the top of her forehead in slow, patient motions, as if it had a mind of its own. He inched closer to her face, sitting on the edge of her bed, and recited the last poem she had circled in his William Blake anthology, before she lost her voice and will to speak.

O Rose thou art sick.
The invisible worm,
That flies in the night
In the howling storm:

Has found out thy bed
Of crimson joy:
And his dark secret love
Does thy life destroy.

The last word, destroy, collected at his lips and came out in a garbled sob, his fragile body, made of teetering bones held together by string and glue, trembling into hers as he fell upon her own fading flesh.

"I'm sorry, darling," he whispered into her ear, collecting and lifting himself away from her with a gentle push of his hands from the pillows that propped her head up. "Maybe this was not the best poem to read to you, but it is your favorite, and it just really speaks to this moment. Your illness. Our life together as it has become."

He waited for her reply, some sign that it was alright, that he hadn't reminded her of her dying flesh, her fading life. That he had chosen the right poem to put her in the right mood. That he had made her happy, for that is all he wanted to do until the last moment, the moment she left him for good.

"Please forgive me," he cried into her eyes.

Transfixed, he clung to her for signs of approval, contentment, and he didn't let go of her gaze until he saw a slight tremble on her lips. She was trying to smile.

"Oh, good. Thank you, precious. My rose. My sick, sick rose." He straightened and heaved a deep sigh that ballooned his belly and seemed to take up the entire room.

"It's time for bed, don't you think?" He asked her, grinning in her direction as he took off his trousers and shirt and placed them at the edge of the bed. As he walked around to his side, he folded himself into the covers, still dressed in undershirt, boxer shorts, and socks. He hated the feel of his toes without socks, the grating sensation of anything getting stuck on his toenails was like an aggravating assault to his nerves, so he never took them off. Not even in bed.

Under the covers, he faced his wife, and slowly turned her to him, wanting her eyes to be the last things he saw before falling asleep. She looked back at him and smiled. He smiled back, feeling full and happy with love for this wonderful woman who had chosen him for life. He took hold of her hand and placed it on his chest, and they both fell asleep to the beat of his heart beating into her hand, an audible thumping sound that connected them even in sleep.

CHAPTER 6

"He's not right, Camilla. In the head." Chelsea sat opposite Camilla at their usual spot in the Library Cafe, tucked inside the Lucy Scribner Library on the college campus. They each had a class to get to and only twenty minutes to drink their coffee and catch up between academic runs. "There are rumors about him. The way he looks at girls. Some of them have complained about it. Don't you feel the creeps around him?"

"The creeps?" Camilla's throaty laugh rang out to the other side of the cafe, students glancing over their laptops and notebooks with curiosity.

"Yeah, the creeps," Chelsea repeated, lines of concern outlining the forehead Camilla loved to run her fingers across. There was something about Chelsea's forehead skin. It was smooth and flawless, and Camilla loved caressing it, smoothing the worry away. She wanted to touch it now but knew not to with Chelsea's fiery mood at play. Her friend would not appreciate being touched at this moment. She had too much to say to her about Carl's strangeness. "Honey, I'm worried about you. That's all. I don't mean to be a killjoy."

"I know, Chelsea. I'm not going to replace you with Carl. Promise."

"Is that what you think this is about? Camilla, I'm not feeling insecure because you're in a relationship. You know me better than that. I just get these strange vibes coming from him. I can't explain it. He reminds me of my father."

Camilla reached across the table to grab her friend's fingers and intertwine them into her own.

"I'm sorry. I didn't mean to be condescending. But Carl is not your father. He doesn't drink. He doesn't hurt women. He's kind and good, and he makes me feel present in my body. I've never felt that way with a man before. In fact, I'm the only serious relationship he's had in a long time, Chelsea. I think I love him." The last words came out in a hoarse whisper and her voice caught in her throat. She had never said those words aloud before about a man. Only to Chelsea. To her father, the day before she had him buried in the lot beside her mother, so they could rest together, side by side, since her death had taken her out of their lives when Camilla was only twelve. They were together now, back in New England, and Camilla had not returned to the roots she had left behind.

"Camilla?" Chelsea's voice brought her back.

"Sorry. I was thinking about my father. It's ironic," she laughed, "but Carl reminds me of him. He was quiet and lonely and so full of love. That's Carl. I want you to meet him."

"I have met him. I took his British Lit course a semester before you."

"Not that way. Come over for dinner. See him outside of the academic world, when he is dressed casually and not like a professor. That's just his title. But at home, he's soft and likeable and he laughs all the time. Like everything I say is funny."

"Sure," Chelsea conceded. "Maybe one day. Listen, I have to go." She grabbed a glance at her watch and rushed a final sip of her cappuccino into her mouth. "I have to run across the Quad."

"Okay," Camilla sighed, feeling like things were not resolved between them. Maybe it would just take time. "I'll walk outside with you."

"Will I see you tonight? At our apartment? You know, you still live there." She tried to throw her friend a casual smile, but it came out tight and forced.

"I don't know. Probably not. I may stay over Carl's tonight." Camilla looked at her friend, facing her, her blond hair whipping about her small features from the force of the wind enveloping them. She reached out, grabbed a wisp of the pale tendrils, and tucked them behind Chelsea's ear, pierced in three places with the star, moon, and sun earring buds twinkling in the sunlight.

"You've been sleeping over his place for a week now. Are you going to move in with him?" Chelsea asked, her pale blue eyes boring into her dark ones with a silent warning she hoped Camilla would understand without words.

Camilla inhaled deeply at the thought and released a sigh. "I don't know. Maybe. Would you be okay with that?"

"I'm not your keeper, Camilla." Chelsea heard the coldness in her voice, caught the slight wince in Camilla's eyes, and adjusted her bag over her shoulders. "I love you. I support you. I'm always here for you. I just don't want to see you get hurt." This time her tone was soft, and she had to avert her eyes from meeting Camilla's, knowing she would see pain there, loss even.

"You will not lose me, silly. You're my best friend, my sister. I love you."

"I know. Just be careful, okay. And call me. Let me know if you need anything."

Camilla leaned over to her friend and hugged her, pulling her so close and with such force, both girls shook with laughter at the closeness, gasping for air.

"I'll see you," Chelsea shouted as she ran across the quad, her red pants and white tennis shoes becoming a blurred collage of colors as the distance yawned between them. Feeling a chill along her spine, Camilla turned her face to the sun, welcoming the light and warmth emitting from its rays and slipping into her skin through her pores. She felt full and content. She knew what she would do next, and instead of going to her own art class, she made her way to the parking lot, got into her car, and stepped on the gas, moving in the opposite direction of the school and this phase of her life.

"Let's get married." Camilla nuzzled her nose deep into Carl's neck, inhaling his scent. He always smelled of old leather and spice, the combination reminding her of home, when she used to live with her father. They were lying in his enormous bed, two crumpled, naked bodies tightly coiled around each other in the middle of the lumpy mattress, a thin beige sheet covering all but their arms and hands.

Carl clucked his tongue at her. "We've only just met, you know. I haven't even met your parents. Don't you think they will want to meet me first?"

"My parents are both dead," she said, tucking her head against the full bed of gray hair on his chest.

"I'm sorry. I didn't know." He kissed the top of her head and pulled her closer to him.

When she said nothing, he prodded.

"What happened to them?"

She sighed, then pried her face off his chest and leaned back so her eyes rested in his. "My mother killed herself when I was twelve. I found her in the garage, in her car. It looked like she was sleeping. So peaceful. But when I yelled at her and knocked on the window to wake her up, she wouldn't. I tried opening the door, but it was locked from the inside. As if she didn't want anyone to go in there with her. Or after her. When the ambulance came and took her away, they found a container of sleeping pills on the floor of the car. It was empty."

"I'm so sorry," he mumbled into her dark hair, squeezing her shoulder with wide fingers that made her feel like she could lean into them even farther. She did. She sank into them and they held her up, carrying the weight of her as if it did not come with baggage and despair.

"Funny thing is, I remember my father talking to me about it all a few hours later, tucking me into bed. He told me she had just been tired and needed to sleep. She hadn't been able to. Sleep, I mean. So, she kept taking the pills, one after the other, hoping the more she took, the more sleep she would get, and she lost track. But I didn't believe him. Who would try to sleep in the car? In the middle of the day?"

"How about your father? How did he pass?"

"He died of lymphoma a few years ago. I went home, took care of the funeral arrangements, sold the house I grew up in, and never returned. There's nothing for me there, except memories of broken people. Both of them were broken."

"What makes you say that?"

"Well, she was broken to want to kill herself. She had a child. That's just selfish. To kill yourself and leave behind a child. She never even left me a note. No explanation. Nothing. And my dad, he was broken after her suicide. He was there, he took me to school, he showed up at my dance recitals, he met my boyfriends, but he really wasn't present. It was always quiet between us. Our dinners were without noise, except for the sound of utensils hitting plates or glasses being moved or picked up and put down again. We had one conversation, after my mother died, and then there was nothing. It's like he raised me because he had to, but there was nothing between us. No words. No love. Just layers and layers of uncomfortable quiet."

"It must have been very lonely for you." Carl's voice was low and gruff, pulling her gaze to his.

"Yes. I was very lonely. But it taught me not to expect anything from anyone. It taught me to be comfortable in my skin, in my aloneness."

"Are you lonely still?" Camilla could feel the smile on his mouth as it rested on the top of her head, his breathing sending chills through her scalp.

"I'm not lonely now, Carl. You fill all the emptiness inside me with love. And poetry." She giggled at this last point, since they both knew that every time he read her a poem from one of those "dead white guys," as she so often referred to them, she dozed off.

He chuckled, a deep rumble that vibrated from his chest cavity into hers, resting there as if it had found its home. She moved then, sliding out from the crook of his arm and climbing onto his lap, straddling him in place while her fingers cupped his face. She touched her forehead to his.

"So, let's get married. I have no one but you. And you have no one but me. Let's be everything and everyone to each other."

"Yes," he said, gently pressing his lips to hers. "But on one condition."

"What's that?" She shifted her hips slightly, so that they grazed over his growing erection, and she licked her lips, tasting him as his eyes took on that nebulous look that spoke of desire and hunger she entrusted only him to feed.

Carl pushed her away so he could get his words out. "You say you have no one, but this is not true. You have Chelsea. And she distrusts me. I see her walking past my office door on campus almost daily. She never talks to me, but she's there, watching me. We need to have her over for dinner. So she can see that I'm not a villain in your story. I'm not trying to get between the two of you. If she sees us together, maybe she'll offer her blessing."

"Sounds good, Professor. Now shut up and ravish me," she whispered into his ear, taking the lobe into her mouth and biting it for good measure.

He let out a growl, grabbed her from behind, and positioned himself above her, the entirety of his body, wide and thick with pleasure, crushing hers into submission. And Camilla surrendered all of herself to him.

CHAPTER 7

Camilla winked at her friend over the chicken cordon bleu that Carl placed on the table between them. Steam rose from the roasted asparagus he added to the line of food already sprinkled about the weathered cherry-lacquered table in Carl's homey kitchen.

"You can't tell me he's not a find. A man who enjoys cooking," she murmured heavily into the open space between them, beaming at her friend.

"Um, yeah. It's lovely, being fed. I haven't had a meal like this since I left home five years ago," Chelsea admitted, her eyes gliding over the dishes, her fingers itching to grab at the food. She pushed back the impulse by taking in her surroundings instead. The kitchen was a wall of wood, heavy oak. The only light that broke through the dark blanket covering the small kitchen came from the streetlight peeking through the small window above the sink and the dusted chandelier that hung low above the table they had gathered, about to eat.

"Dig in, ladies." Carl took off his plain white apron and hung it over the back of his chair. He handed the platter of chicken to Camilla on his right and then the bowl of asparagus to Chelsea on his left. He watched them fill their plates with food and smiled, recalling the college year hungers of his own youth, how cherished it had been when someone had invited him over for a home-cooked meal. Once he had returned to this house, his childhood home, and began to live in it, he had cooked all his meals here, in this kitchen, never needing to go out for dinners that he could put together with his own ingredients, his own hands. Eating had been a pleasure for him, but now, having two young women in his home, stuffing their faces with food he had prepared for them, was even better. There was another, more visceral level of pleasure that unleashed itself inside of him. It made his heart ache with longing, and he pushed back the desire to feed them himself, to grab their forks and take turns placing bits of chicken and vegetable into their mouths one by one. Like a father. Like a feeder of wants. But he held back his urges, the impulses he spent years cultivating and controlling, and he watched them instead, a satisfied grin fixed on his mouth.

"We're getting married!" Camila flung the words into the air with careless abandon, giggling at her friend. The one member of her tribe.

"You're what?" Chelsea's hand froze in mid-air, as did the fork with asparagus clinging to it on its way into her mouth. "Married?" She looked at her friend, a frown of uneven lines overtaking the surface of her forehead. She already felt a migraine building up behind her eyes, blinding her, blurring the vision of her smiling friend and the older man who looked bewildered sitting opposite her.

"Yes. Married."

"Camilla, you've only known him for a few months. You know nothing about him." Chelsea knew she was being rude and out of line, but this was too much for her.

"Please excuse me. I'll let you ladies talk," Carl muttered, his cheeks pink. But just as he was about to rise from his chair, Camilla grabbed his arm and pulled him back down.

"No, Carl. Stay." She turned to Chelsea then, her eyes dark and humorless.

"Chelsea," she began, her voice soft but with a hardness in it that Chelsea had never heard before. "I love him. I love you, too, but if you keep going against my wishes, there will be no room for you in my life. And I want you in my life. I want you at my wedding, standing beside me as my maid of honor. I want you with me when I have my babies, and I want you to be a Godmother to them. To watch out for them as you have watched out for me. I don't need a mother. I need my friend. What do you say?"

They locked eyes, silently debating their options, so they didn't notice the sweat trickling down Carl's cheeks or the bulbous distress in his own eyes, as his right hand flailed in the air. It was only when his other arm, the free one, hit the table's surface with a sharp bang that the two women drew their attention to him.

"Carl!" Camilla screamed, catching him in time as he slipped out of his chair. "Call for an ambulance," she shot the command at Chelsea without looking at her, Carl's head cradled in her arms, both of them sprawled on the floor.

"C'mon, Professor. Stay with me. You got that?"

* * *

A few months after Carl's mini stroke, Camilla and Carl married. It was a minor affair that took place in Carl's backyard, amid red and white rose bushes and pink azaleas. Camilla wore a simple beige dress she found in a thrift store, and Carl put on his best suit. A local minister officiated the ceremony, and Chelsea, the Maid of Honor, signed the marriage license as the only other witness to the bond.

After they ate the wedding cake Chelsea had brought from the local bakery, Carl walked Chelsea to her car.

"I still don't trust you," Chelsea's sea-blue eyes took hold of Carl's with force. His hazel ones did not waver in hers. He let himself be consumed and disarmed.

"I know you don't, Chelsea. But it's alright. I'm glad Camilla has such a loyal friend in you. You're always welcome here."

"I'm not going anywhere." Her words came out harsher than she intended, but she didn't back down. "I'm watching you, Professor."

As her car rolled out of the gravel driveway, she caught sight of his face in the rear-view mirror. He was looking back at her, smiling. A chill slithered up and down her spine, like a snake circling her throat and then squeezing all the air out of her.

CHAPTER 8

"I have a surprise for you."

Carl grabbed hold of Camilla's hand and pulled her out of bed. She dressed quickly and let him lead her out of the bedroom they had been spending much of their time in, making love. It was their honeymoon week, and instead of traipsing around the country, they stayed home, moved her in, and nested. At least Camilla wanted to nest. While he spent his hiatus from work tending to his vegetable garden in the back, Camilla tried to soften the hard edges of the home she was to share with Carl for the rest of her life. She bought light blue ornamental pillows for the living room couch and found floor lamps at antique shops that would lighten the spaces of her new home. It was always so dark, so austere in the rooms that should have been lit by the yawning sunlight struggling to slip in through the break in the curtains. She replaced his old curtains, heavy and dark gray, with sheer ones that welcomed the light and let it pass through. They met in the bedroom at midday, to make love, and then lay in bed, talking and eating cheese and crackers from a tray Carl had brought in prior to their entangling.

Carl was elated, charmed by the young girl in his bed, in his home, the way she came in with brightness following her and staying with her. She made everything light and surreal, and it wasn't until she had made the changes in his home that he realized how darkly he had been living.

How lonely he had been. Even his heart, which had been sitting in his cavity chest like a heavy stone, had buoyed to the surface, as if someone had placed a life preserver around it. He felt it dancing against his chest, a waltz that made him glide to his garden every morning, awaiting the moment that they would tumble into bed and he could show her the depths of his love for her.

"I have a gift for you." His words enticed her to follow him up the stairs to the attic.

Camilla giggled, a series of bells trickling into his ears and planting seeds of blossoms in his already lightened heart.

He opened the attic door and leaned against it, watching her face to locate the expressions he anticipated growing there like flowers. He wasn't disappointed in what he found there. A smile, wide and full, tears glistening in the eyes that opened and closed in rapture when he lay above her, his own gaze riveted to her as if she had put a spell on him. He enjoyed pleasing her. In bed. With food. And even now.

He watched as Camilla's gaze took in what used to be a small room with a wall of dirty and crusted windows. The light couldn't even seep through the stains of neglect and grime. But now they were washed, and they gleamed in the sunlight. The room was also cleaned out. All the old furniture that had been stocked and locked in there for decades—tables, chairs, broken lamps, all full of dust and decay—were removed. They had taken up so much of the attic space, but now that they were missing from the scene, the attic space looked open and larger than one had expected.

In the middle of the room stood a brand-new easel, and beside it a table filled with acrylic paints of all shades imaginable. The wall on the far right was peppered with sheets of paper and canvases, bare and white, waiting to be imprinted with images that still rested in her mind. She moved closer to the easel, a bare canvas already in the room's center and facing the arched bay of windows that revealed a painting of its own. There was the sun already drawn against a crystal blue sky and a floor of green grass leading to a wall of trees swaying against the breeze, a slow, soothing motion that made no sound but lulled one to a place of calm and peace.

"Carl," she whispered. "What did you do with all the furniture from this room? When did you do all this?"

He smiled, pleased in finding the joy he sought in her eyes, on her mouth, already red with pleasure. It's one of the first things he noticed about her. She didn't wear makeup. Her skin was alabaster white, and the contrast of her dark eyes and hair against it made his insides stir with excitement. But when she was excited, lustful and desirous, her mouth turned red and voluptuous against the frame of her pale skin. She looked like a vampire, a beautiful, dark, wondrous thing that haunted his dreams, waking him up in the middle of the night to discover her lying beside him, serene, snoring slightly in her sleep. He would touch her then, run his fingers along her chest cavity, cup her breasts, lift her t-shirt, and follow the trail down to her cervical bone. He slipped his fingers inside her panties until he reached the bed of wetness that waited for him. Only for him. His fingers played her body like a pianoforte, his eyes glued to her face, watching for stirrings of desire he had planted in her garden. When she moaned in her sleep, he moved over her and made love to her, watching her the entire time, wanting nothing more than to meet her eyes when she woke up during her orgasm to find him on top of her, inside of her, the one and only cause of her derived pleasure. Just thinking about all the nights he had loved her to submission, to rapture, to wakefulness, turned him on. He wanted nothing more than to push the paints and brushes she was admiring off the table and take her again and again until she was so full of him there would be no room for anything else in her.

"Carl?" Her soft voice brought him back to the attic, to the table he was eyeing, imagining her on its hard surface, bare and wanting.

He coughed his desire back in place and ran his gaze over hers. "Mostly at night. When I couldn't sleep. I donated most of the furniture, moved some to the garage, or broke and burned the decayed ones out in the back. You did not know?"

"No. I guess Chelsea is right about me. I'm clueless. You've been doing all this for me, with me in the house, and I had no idea." She moved toward him and touched his cheek with her long, ringed fingers. He felt a coldness replace the heat of her touch when she pulled her body away from his and sauntered across the small space of the room to the windows. She leaned against the glass and dragged her gaze to his, eyeing him, a playful smirk growing about her lips.

"I guess there's only one more thing we need to do." Her voice was husky when it reached him, still standing by the door, and it sounded to him like a siren's call, bringing him to attention, the hairs on his arms standing tall and vibrating toward the sound of her voice.

"What's that?"

Camilla didn't answer him. She only smiled in that coy way of hers that told him what she had in mind. And then, just to show him, she faced the windows, pressing her face and chest into them. With one arm splayed against the glass pane, almost as if she were grabbing it, Camilla reached behind her with the other arm, her fingers lifting the white miniskirt she was wearing, over her buttocks, until the fabric and her fingers clasped the back of her waist. She wasn't wearing any underwear, and the sight of her bare bottom, now pushing away from the glass windows, toward him, grinding in slow motion as if waiting for him to touch it, caused a hardness in him. Desire spilled out of his mouth in a groan, low and thick and wild, like the sounds a pained animal makes.

He lunged for her, almost knocking down the easel in his quest for her, his eyes still drawn to the circular movements of her bottom, the small moans escaping her lips and pulling him to her. He didn't realize he was holding his breath until his body made contact with hers and he pushed himself inside of her, releasing a sigh only when he was taken by her warmth and the love that lived there.

And as he made love to her from behind, his teeth biting the soft skin on her neck, his hands cupping the bare buds of her breasts, he realized this was how he wanted to die. Inside her. Where it was all warm and wet and comforting, all of her taking him in with such ease, such wantonness. There was no other place he wanted to be except in all the hidden places of her body that made him feel loved and desired and complete. And safe.

CHAPTER 9

Camilla sat opposite her best friend at an old cafe around the corner of Skidmore College, sipping the foam off her cappuccino and picking at the nuts sprinkled atop her blueberry muffin placed in front of her.

Chelsea looked tired. Eyes that had always shone like blue lightning about to strike from their orbs seemed dull now. Pained somehow. Camilla hoped this dullness had not been her doing. Friendships always changed when love came calling, and Carl had filled most of the voids that had lived inside her. Almost all of them. There were some holes too deep and too damaged to fill completely. And that was not Carl's doing. That was just her damage. Her brokenness.

"You look tired," Camilla observed, popping a lone nut into her mouth and chewing on it.

"I am, a bit." Chelsea let out a laugh so small that Camilla almost missed it. She watched Chelsea shake off her dark mood as if it were as easy as peeling off a scarf from around her neck. "How are you? How's married life?"

"Delicious," Camilla purred, retrieving a laugh from her friend's mouth. "Carl's older, but seriously, Chelsea. He's the best lover I've ever had. I don't know why I wasted so much time on the young ones. They're just learning. Carl is thorough and passionate and just a pleasure at pleasing me." She sighed aloud, sitting back in her chair and closing her eyes against the onslaught of the sun striking them from above.

"That's great," Chelsea smiled over her iced chai latte. They were sitting outside, and it was too hot to drink anything else. She also needed the ice chunks in her drink to chew on, anticipating the confession she had to make to her friend. "I'm glad you're happy."

Chelsea cleared her throat. "I haven't seen you on campus lately, though. Are you taking a break?"

"I decided not to continue with school. And before you go off the bend, Chelsea, I just have to say, school's not for me. Not right now. Carl cleared out the attic space for me and filled it with easels, bare canvasses, and paints. And I am painting again. Like really painting. The kind I haven't been able to paint in years. I feel so free and unencumbered, and all these images are flashing in my thoughts— behind my eyes. And my hands just take over. You know? It's an incredible feeling. I'm done with school for now. I just want to paint. And make love to Carl. And make a home with him."

Chelsea pushed down the feelings of resistance laboring for release from the tough layers of her skin, knowing that the more she pushed, the further she would push her friend in the opposite direction. Away from her. And there was already too much distance between them now that Carl had found a way in. She just smiled and told Camilla she was happy for her.

"Are you, really? It means so much to me to have your support." Camilla reached out to place her fingers on top of Chelsea's pale ones.

"I am. As long as you're happy, I'm happy. But I have something to tell you, too. I'm leaving."

"What do you mean?" Camilla pulled her hand back as if Chelsea's skin burned.

"I was offered a fellowship at Columbia's school of arts. I can't turn it down. It's an amazing opportunity to grow as a painter, and there's an amazing teacher there who can help me advance. So, I am leaving Skidmore, too. I guess it's become a dead end for both of us." She smiled weakly at her friend, feeling tears about to fill the corners of her eyes.

"Oh, Chelsea. Don't cry. This is good. I'm moving on. You're moving up. We're both pursuing our art. Promise me you'll keep in touch, though. That you won't disappear from me."

"Never. I'll always be only one phone call away. You know that. And," a mischievous twinkle appeared in her eyes. "Who will be here to remind you that Carl is a tab bit of a weirdo?"

"Oh, my God, Chelsea." Camilla was in mid-sip of her drink and almost spit it out. "I wish you were sticking around to get to know him better. He's love, Chelsea. Pure love. And I want to have his babies. Like lots of them. So please be kind when talking about the future father of my children."

"Yes, I gathered children would come next. I think it's what you've always wanted. A home, a partner, a child or two."

"Or ten. Oh, just the idea of children running around that big house fills me with joy. I would make an exceptional mother, don't you think?"

Chelsea nodded her head. "I do. I think you will make a wonderful mother."

There was a pause between them. Not one of those uncomfortable marks of time that everyone eyed and tried to avoid. But one of those breaks of sound that was full of eyes locking with understanding. With words neither woman could muster to fill the yawning space between them. But they didn't need to. They knew how the other felt. They were sisters, after all.

"When are you leaving?" Camilla asked, taking the last sip from her drink.

"Tomorrow. I'm staying with a friend until I find a place, but I feel like there's nothing here for me now. So why not go as quickly as possible?"

I'm still here, Camilla wanted to say but didn't. She let the words rest between them silently. She didn't want to open another topic that she was sure would force Chelsea to tell her what she really thought. Camilla knew Chelsea's thoughts. She mistrusted Carl.

"I'll miss you, Chels." Camilla noted the forced smile on her friend's lips at that. Chelsea wasn't the kind of girl to keep silent, but Camilla could see that she was almost choking on the words she was forcing back down her throat.

"You got my number," Chelsea reminded her. "If you need me, you know how to reach me. Love you." Chelsea slipped her body into Camilla's for a tight hug, squeezing the bubble of unsaid things between them and hoping it wouldn't burst.

Chelsea was smart, Camilla thought to herself as she walked in the opposite direction, toward the home and life she shared with Carl. She knew nothing would deter Camilla from loving Carl all the way through, even if it led down a disastrous path, which she doubted would happen. Carl was a keeper. And she was willing to part with friendship to a woman for that longer and deeper connection to a man. Especially a man like Carl, who loved her like a father and a lover combined. She found both qualities in him, and although the father-lover dyad could be disturbing for someone like Chelsea, Camilla knew what she needed. She had always been looking for a man who would embody both, someone who would take care of her, love her, and please her at the same time.

This was what had been missing in her love affairs with the other men of her past. They had loved her body, kissed her mouth, but they had never loved the girl that scratched her nails against her insides for nurturance. These men did not want to know about the girl—they only saw the woman and how her body could serve them, exist merely to fulfill their carnal desires. Carl saw the girl and the woman, and he loved them both—at the same time. His tenderness was immeasurable, uncontainable, and he had enough for all the unmet needs that had existed before him. For now, Carl was all she needed. It was hard watching Chelsea walk away from her and out of her life. The space she left behind was cold and palpable, but her future lay in Carl. In the warmth he provided that she could nestle into without fear of absence or loss.

Thinking of him, of his arms around her, it was with great difficulty that Camilla made it home without sprinting, a grin as deep and full as her heart felt painted on her mouth.

Home. Home was where Carl waited for her, his arms open, his lungs inhaling the lilac scents tangled in her hair after, his coffee and cigarette breath fanning against her cheek when he reached down to kiss her, his hands knowing the needs of her body without her having to ask or say or speak them. He knew. Had always known.

And she knew him, too. His needs, his predilections, without him ever having to ask or say a word.

Camilla understood his need to love her in the dark, in the middle of the night, when she was fast asleep. But she had always been a light sleeper, and the first time she felt him touching her while asleep, she had awakened to find his head over her breasts, his fingers inside her. She lay still that first night and all the nights thereafter. The idea of him loving her without her knowing it mesmerized her, and she pretended to be asleep just so she could discover his needs, the wants he was too afraid to ask for when they were awake. This was him asking, while she slept, and pretending to sleep as he slipped himself inside her body was her way of saying yes. Her body belonged to him as much as it belonged to her, and there was something wondrous and dark and extraordinary about a man loving her body as if she were not in it. She didn't have to respond, to kiss him back, to confirm her pleasure with a moan. She only had to lie there, with her eyes closed, breathing heavily as in sleep, and feel his hands and fingers and mouth on her skin, waking to him with her eyes open only when orgasm overtook her, and she could no longer conceal her awareness. Who could sleep through that, anyway?

As tender as he was, there was also a roughness to his touch, the way his fingers jammed inside her that made her whole sex burn with desire and she wanted to grab his hair with her own fingers, yank his head, and fuck him back with equal force. But she did that later in the day, when it was her turn to play with him, with his body, feeding her own hungers with the force and power she enjoyed. In the middle of the night, in the dark, when he thought she was asleep, she let him have her body in his way, in the way he needed it to feed him.

This was love. A give and a take. A push and a pull. Seeing the holes and the needs and feeding them in any way necessary. It's what we do for the ones we love, even the dark ones who lie awake in the middle of the night and take what they want in secret.

CHAPTER 10

A knock on the door brought Carl back to the present. He realized he had fallen asleep on the living room chair, his legs propped up against the coffee table between him and the bay window speckled with dust and cobwebs. One of these days, he thought to himself, he would clean. If only his hips didn't burn and his hands didn't shake whenever he attempted to tidy the place up a bit, make it homier and more comfortable.

"What does it matter, anyway?" He snickered aloud, startled by the sound of his own voice filling up the quiet spaces of his home. It's not like anyone else was around. Camilla was upstairs, in her bed, sleeping. She never came down here. She wasn't able to, and he could no longer carry her down the stairs, as he used to, laying her on the couch and sitting beside her, pulling her feet onto his lap and caressing the finely curved bones of her toes. He was too weak now. Too many mini strokes upset his equilibrium, and one more stroke, the doctors had told him, would do him in. And he believed them. He didn't care anymore about dying. As long as he was with Camilla, that is all that mattered. Dying in her arms would be the only way to go, the best way. But who would take care of her then?

He shook his head in dismay. He had to keep on. For her. To keep her safe.

The bell rang this time, jarring him from his thoughts.

"Alright. I'm coming," he hollered at the door, his feet forcing him across the room in slow, tedious movements that made him ache all over.

"Who is it?" He asked this at the same time he swung the door open, coming face to face with the woman he hadn't expected to see ever again.

"Hi, Carl." The woman standing before him was in her forties, her blond hair bunched up in a tidy knot atop her head. Her eyes, blue and sharp, reminded him of open skies and the youthfulness that he could no longer hold in the palm of his hand. They were both fleeting and transient, as was the woman who stood before him, small and proud, stubbornness written all along the lines that scrunched up the loosened skin on her forehead. Chelsea was beautiful, still, while his wife was a crumpled and decaying body only one floor above them.

"Chelsea, how are you? What are you doing here?" His voice was gruff and hoarse as the words exited his mouth. Gruffer than he had intended.

"I was in the neighborhood and thought I'd come for a visit. I tried calling the old number, but I kept getting the wrong people."

"Yes," he nodded his head. "We got rid of the phone a long time ago. No use for it."

They stood at the doorway for what seemed like an interminable number of seconds until Carl remembered his manners and moved his shriveled bones to the side, waving her into the house with shaky fingers.

"Have a seat," Carl motioned to a spot on the couch in the middle of the living room. He turned on a lamp sitting on the table between them, hoping it would give the room a brighter appearance. It didn't help much. It only highlighted the austere and abandoned look of the place. The layers of dust on furniture and books and bookcases, the worn and sunken fabric of the couches and chairs that no one had sat upon for years, the neglected windowpanes covered in grime that refused to let sunlight burst through its thick layers, and the dilapidated staircase that led to the dark regions of the upstairs bedrooms.

Chelsea's eyes took in the scene before her, including the much older man whose labored steps reminded her of old people scuffling along floors, leaning on canes and walkers for balance. She took a seat on the corner of the dusty couch, clenched her purse to her chest, and tried to pacify the uneasy feeling that overcame her.

"Would you like something to drink? Perhaps tea or water?" Carl offered the woman who still resembled the outspoken girl he had once known.

"No," she shook her head with vigorous force. Chelsea did not want anything from this place touching her lips or going into her system. She imagined grime on glasses this man could no longer see, and the thought of putting her lips on any object from this house made her stomach churn involuntarily. "I can't stay. My husband is waiting for me with our sons at the bookstore on Main Street. While they were in there, I thought I'd drive by to see if you and Camilla still lived here. I'm so glad I found you." She let out a nervous laugh, noting that she didn't mean him, but Camilla.

"Yes, we never left. This was home. For both of us."

"Is Camilla around? Can I see her? I can't stay long, but I wanted to see her one last time, I suppose. We're driving back to North Carolina today."

"Is that home for you, then?"

"Yes. It's been home for ten years now, since we had the boys. Twins. Joseph and Michael. They keep me quite busy, and I feel bad I haven't been better at keeping in touch with Camilla."

"Pft," Carl waved her worries away with a swipe of his freckled hand. "Camilla loves you. She was happy when she learned about your marriage and boys. She always wanted you to find your place and happiness. And she was busy herself, you know. We live our lives and move on, and at least you're here now. It's good to see you, Chelsea."

"Yes," Chelsea's chin lowered with guilt. "I'm sorry I wasn't around for her. But I'm glad that she has you."

"Yes. I'm sorry she never had children. It's what she wanted most in our life together." A tear welled up in his eye and slipped down his cheek. His left hand trembled like a tiny quake as it brought a skeletal finger up to his face to wipe it away. "My only regret is not being able to give her what she most desired. A home full of children. She's been so lonely without them. It's an emptiness I haven't been able to fill for her."

"Oh, Carl," Chelsea began and then stopped, afraid to sound patronizing or condescending. There were no words to offer to him for the losses he and Camilla had encountered, and she almost felt guilty with two sons of her own, the sounds and chaos of child noises filling her home and life for ten years now. She looked around the interior of the house her friend had once loved and made her own, finding no evidence of her friend in it. Or evidence of cheer or happiness. It was a decayed home, a gloomy one. Is this what happens to homes that suffer loss and childlessness? Chelsea kept the thought to herself.

She eyed the man sitting opposite her in a weathered brown leather chair that she recalled teasing Camilla about, how it matched the leather patch on the elbows of his old and tattered jackets. The man before her now was not someone to tease about or laugh at. Sadness sloped his back and lined his face with an interminable array of wrinkles concealing the freckles Camilla had loved to point to, reminding Chelsea of the boyishness which had once played on his features. There was no evidence of boyishness in him, Chelsea thought to herself. It seemed to her as if he were just waiting to die in this home that had once shone with light and vibrated with life.

"So, where is Camilla?" She smiled tentatively at the man observing her with curiosity. "Can I see her? I have to get back soon. I won't stay long. I just wanted to lay my eyes on her, see if she's alright."

"Let me check on her." Carl readied himself to rise from the chair holding his sunken body, and Chelsea felt the inclination to jump up and help him, but something in the way he looked at her glued her to her spot.

"Thanks, Carl," was all she said, her voice almost a murmur.

She watched as he disappeared into the shadows of the staircase, the only sounds coming from the creaking of his bones as he climbed the stairs, the wood beneath his steps moaning in response to the slight weight he put on them to push himself forward.

She wondered how he had gotten to look so old, so unattended to. Only twenty years had passed since she had known him, which would put him in his late 70s. But he wore the wear and tear of a dying man. It must have been the mini strokes he had, she thought, nodding her head as she recalled the letters Camilla had written to her during the early years after she had left Saratoga Springs. When they had both been in their late twenties. The letters had halted when they were both around thirty-five. Camilla had just suffered a miscarriage and had written to her about it, about the loneliness she felt, the burden of being unable to carry a baby to term, of failing Carl and herself, of never knowing the gifts that would come with motherhood. Chelsea had written back a few times, trying to pacify the negative feelings that overrode those letters and her friend's life, but she had not heard back from her. And at that point, she had been pregnant herself and unable to share the news with her friend.

A woman losing babies doesn't want to hear about another woman's fertility and success in birthing children. Children that grow to full term and come out of her body, pushing their way through to the light. Children swept up, wailing and wet, placed in their mother's arms. A woman who cannot experience these parts because her body isn't working does not want to hear any of it. She would rather you just kept it to yourself. So Chelsea kept it to herself. And when she didn't hear back from Camilla, she just assumed Camilla had finished with her, had committed herself to Carl even more now that children would never be an option. She had let go of the only other woman she had ever loved, out of kindness, out of respect, not wanting to shove her happiness in the face of a woman who could not have what had come so easily to her.

Before Chelsea knew it, ten years had passed, and her twins had filled the parts Camilla had abandoned. They had been enough for her. Until she had brought them to Saratoga Springs to show them her school and the paintings the art gallery on Main Street had recently commissioned from her. A local artist, they had advertised, with her full name in the article, even though she hadn't been back in twenty years. While she was here, she had to see if she could reconnect with Camilla. Maybe even pick up where they had left off. Be friends again. Share their lives again.

Her thoughts were interrupted by the sound of wood creaking and cracking, then feet scuffling across the floorboards. She looked up to find Carl standing a few feet away from her, his fingers trembling in the air, in perfect tempo to his shaking head.

"She's sleeping still," Carl told her, sinking into the chair opposite hers, its leather fabric torn and resembling a series of spider webs overtaking its surface. "I tried to wake her. She would love to see you, but she took a pain killer an hour ago, and it knocked her out."

"Oh," Chelsea mouthed, unable to hide her disappointment. "Is she in a lot of pain?"

"Yes. Almost always when she's awake. The doctors say there's nothing they can do for her. It was either wait to die in a hospital or at home. So, I brought her home. Where I can take care of her."

"You're a good partner, Carl. I'm glad she has you." Chelsea forced a smile and raised her eyes to meet his. They were gray and dull, not as playful as they used to be when he taught his poets in class or over the dinner he had cooked for them so many years ago. There was only pain in them now. She could see it, it was so palpable, so raw. She felt sorry for him suddenly and wished she had not made herself so obvious all those years ago when she had gazed upon him with coldness, doubting his kindness, his sincerity.

He was still creepy, the way his eyes traveled over her face and body, as if he could see more in her than she wanted anyone to see. So was the home that he lived in. But maybe it was his age, his tiredness, the way he dragged his shoes across the unswept wood of the floorboards between them that made her lay her instincts aside for the moment. Maybe he wasn't all that bad. Maybe she was just jealous of the man who had robbed her of her friend, had taken all of Camilla from her, leaving behind only scraps of memories of the girl she had known and loved and the few phone calls between them that stopped altogether after she had left Saratoga Springs for a life she would lead without her sister by her side.

She sighed, unable to suppress her disappointment. "Are you sure I can't just go upstairs and peek in on her?" She asked Carl, trying to hold back the urge to run up the stairs anyway, no matter what his answer would be. That was the earliest lesson Camilla had taught her when they had known each other and lived together.

"Ask for forgiveness but never for permission," Camilla used to sing to her from the bathroom they had shared in their small apartment. Although Chelsea had seemed tough and aggressive, disappointing people around her had been an unacceptable feat for her. She feared losing her friends, the esteem of her professors, the love of the men with whom she had relationships. But when she had left Saratoga Springs and her lovely friend, realizing her role in Camilla's life was in the fading out process, she had remembered her friend's advice when her feet touched the New York City sidewalks. She didn't ask for permission. She collected herself, imprinted a new version of herself onto her skin and identity, and assumed the attitude of someone who would only accept success.

This attitude had gotten her a first showing in a small upscale art gallery in Greenwich Village, and eventually, gallery owners began coming to her, placing their business cards in her hands. And when she saw her future husband, Josh, a cardiologist, on a date in one of her showings, she met his eyes unapologetically. She kissed him by the bathroom stalls while his date watched and stormed out of the place. Chelsea led him to her apartment without caring about anyone else. It was just her and him, and she was a new person who took what she wanted and didn't apologize for it.

But now here she was, waiting in a house she had known from her youth, and her knees trembled at the idea of taking what she wanted. She wanted to climb those stairs, open the door to her friend's bedroom, and sit by her bedside. She wanted to see the eyes of the girl she had loved, the sister she had left behind, and to know that it would be okay for her to leave again, leave her behind. Because that's how it felt to her, surrounded by the decay and debris of old age and neglect. The house itself smelled like it was aging, the stink of moth balls interacting with overripe bananas infusing the air she inhaled each time she took a breath. It was nauseating, sweet and acrid all at the same time. And it was so dark in this home. There was no light coming in and no light going out. She wanted to wipe the grime off the windows and open them just to let life back into this place that housed her friend.

She wondered what her room looked like. If it was just as dark, just as ripe with the stench of sickness.

Carl's gravelly cough grated against her skin, bringing her back to the question she had just asked. "Maybe if you come back another time, she will be awake. If I wake her now, she'll have a hard time sleeping, and I won't be able to give her more pain killers. She'll be awake and in pain."

He paused, noting the grim lines on her mouth, and nodded his head at her. "If you give me advance notice that you'll be coming, I can arrange her schedule so that she's in a good, painless state, and you two can visit. I know she'd love to see you. She hasn't stopped talking about you. I read her the article about your gallery showing a few days ago. She's so very proud of you."

"Alright," Chelsea conceded, not quite happy with his response. The hairs on her arms stood up, and she felt the inclination to run up the stairs, anyway. But this was his house, and she couldn't just push her way into it just because she had a creepy suspicion. So, she shook it off and smiled back at him.

"Well, I do have to come back in a few months to pick up my paintings—the ones that haven't sold. Maybe I can drop by then?"

"Of course. Just drop me a note through the mail, and I'll arrange it so Camilla will be ready for you. Now, if you don't mind, I'm not used to having company. I'm exhausted."

"Yes, yes." Chelsea lifted herself off the couch, brushing her blond hair back and away from her face. Her cheeks flushed pink with embarrassment. She had overstayed her welcome. "I'll let myself out and let you know when I can return. It was good seeing you again, Carl," she lied, slipping her gaze over him so he wouldn't catch the falseness in her voice. "Please tell Camilla I came by. I miss her so."

He nodded his head, his eyes following her across the room and to the door. His eyelids fluttered against his will, like window shutters being pummeled into the wall's foundation by a heavy gust of rain and wind, until Chelsea passed through the threshold and closed the door behind her. He fell into a deep sleep, right there on the brown leather chair, while darkness enfolded him into her arms.

CHAPTER 11

When Carl's eyes opened, it took him a while to get his bearings. He was sitting upright in his chair, the same chair he had in his office at Skidmore College. The college had sent it over to his home after he had retired. Camilla had become ill, and he needed to be at home with her. The college administration had understood. They gave him a party, a healthy retirement package, and even packed his office belongings and sent them over without expecting a dime from him.

The college had been his home, his family. At least before Camilla. He missed his years teaching, standing in front of a room, all eyes on him, ears pricked to hear his musings on poems no one enjoyed reading any more. His courses were full of students each semester, and he believed it was his esteem that brought each year's students to sit before him, willing him to read poetry aloud, his voice deep and throaty, verses vibrating from his lips as if he had been singing to them. That is how he felt, anyway, when he recited poetic lines to his students. As if he was singing to them, lulling them into a place of depth and harmony, where poets and poetry breathed, and life had been renewed for them.

Admittedly, with an embarrassed grin crossing his lips, Carl also missed the young women, their vibrancy, the way they blushed in his presence, gushing about Byron and the articles he had written about the poetry he taught and examined without effort. He had liked the attention, but since Camilla, since the day she had sauntered into his office, demanded his attention, the truth of his awareness of her, the way her eyes ripped him open at the seams and left him gasping for air, like a gutted fish, he had been hooked. He had wanted no other woman except the one who had pressed her breasts against his chest and made him feel like a man for the first time in his life.

His fingers trailed across the leather material of his chair, recalling that first day. This was the chair he had been sitting in when she came on to him, kissed him, and demanded he kiss her back. He had. With everything that was left in him, with every ounce of desire he had repressed all those years, with all these girls flirting with him in his classroom, sticking their pens in their mouths, flicking their tongues over the object they imagined would belong to him. But Camilla had not taunted him, teased him. She had merely taken him. Taken what she wanted and known that he had wanted her back. She gave herself to him without preamble, without the showiness these young girls had pretended at for all the years he had been teaching at Skidmore.

The sound of an object falling to the floor pulled him out of his memories, and he surrendered them with difficulty. He reveled in reshaping the memories that often came to him. Memories of his young Camilla. The healthy one with limber legs and arms that tangled with his during their lovemaking. Carl missed the breathy wisps of air her lungs released into his hair, his ear, moaning beneath him when they became one. He missed the way she tied him up sometimes, his hands and feet bound to the bedposts, her mouth swallowing him whole, orgasming without the ability to grab her, pull her hair back, and cover her mouth with his. He longed for the taste of her when she was young and vibrant. She had often tasted like earth and lilacs and salt all at once.

Carl licked his lips, tasting the memory of her, inhaling the smell of her still embedded in his nostrils. With his eyes closed, he could feel the softness of her skin, the way she succumbed to his touch, his fingers pressing against her throat the way she liked, her eyes growing black with want and desire. Those eyes belonged to him, transformed into that darkness just for him.

Another sound pried his eyes apart again, and this time, he sat up. The noises were coming from upstairs. From Camilla's room. He rose with a start, thinking of the worst that could happen. She could have fallen off the bed in her sleep. Or worse, awakened, lying there in agony, her body splintering with pain, alone, unable to summon him for help.

He quickened his pace along the floor and up the stairs, using the bannister to pull himself up the steps until he made it to the top landing and angled his way into the bedroom they shared. Even after all these years. In sickness and in health.

Carl released a sigh of relief when he saw her in the same position in which he had left her while Chelsea had been visiting. Camilla's head was resting comfortably upon the pillow, her hair, now mousy and dark, lay like a thick vine about her face. She was still lying on her side of the bed, by the window, as if waiting for him to lie beside her, on his side.

He moved to the window and opened it, letting the cool evening breeze flitter into the room and clear out the sticky stench of sickness emanating from her body and preying upon his nostrils, making it difficult for him to breathe.

"It's so muggy in here," he half-spoke to Camilla, not sure she was awake yet. "Now this feels better, no, my darling?" He took in a deep breath, smiling when their eyes met. The old familiar sensation of being consumed by them surged in his gut. She still made him feel things no other human being had ever made him feel. She never failed to surprise him, even now, while she lay in her bed, covered by blankets, unable to move without aches consuming her. Just one look from her catapulted him back to the days she was young and unbroken, virile, her arms clasped around his waist, kissing him with a wantonness no woman had ever expressed for him.

He sat beside her on the bed, careful not to jar her fragile body, looked down at her, and moved a loose strand of hair away from her eyes. No matter how lost he was, how sad and forgotten he felt, he found himself in her. He could see his face and his body in her orbs, as if she were showing him what she saw when she looked at him. And he saw love there, quietly abiding, waiting to capture him, hold him to her in the way her arms no longer had the strength to do so. Tight with desire. With want. She wanted him, even after all this time, all the pain that filled the spaces between them.

"No, my darling. I can't. I don't want to hurt you. You appear so fragile today. I'll just lie beside you and hold you. How's that?" He cupped her chin with his fingers, looking deeply into her eyes so he could convey his love for her. "I want you. I do. But I don't want to hurt you."

He watched her mouth, still lovely and full and inviting, open with protest, even though no sound came out. Her eyes dug into him, conveying her message to him. He understood even without the words. She wanted to feel his love for her, to have him inside her, to be full again.

"Alright, my love. But just let me know if I hurt you. If it's too much for you. You know I want nothing more than to make love to you, but I can't stand it if I hurt you." Tears welled up in his eyes. He clasped her hands in his, bony and thin, cold to the touch, and brought them to his lips.

"You're shivering." He blew warm breaths on her fingers, the way he used to when they had made love outside by the water bank in the back of their house and lay naked afterwards under a blanket of stars. "I'll warm you up, my sick, sick rose."

He moved away then and closed the window, pushing a ream of cold air out of the room and back into the dark, wide expanse of black night that had taken over the sky. Returning to Camilla, he looked into her eyes as he took off his shirt and his pants. His socks stayed on his feet. He locked his eyes with hers, unveiling himself for her, imagining her fingers were the ones undressing him, layer by layer, until he stood over her, naked, desirous of the flesh that would succumb to his touch and the eyes that still played with his.

Sliding the covers away from her body, he parted her robe to reveal the white dressing gown covering the rest of her from him and was bunched up around her hips. He gently lifted her and removed the fabric sandwiched between them. As he positioned himself above her, they were skin on skin now, flesh to flesh, and he felt her tremble beneath him. He kissed her mouth until it was no longer dry, and he felt her soften beneath him. His lips left a trail of wetness from her cheek down to her navel until they rested on her sex, his tongue and fingers taking turns to touch, probe, and enter, rhythmically bringing her to the brink of orgasm and then stopping. When she was ready, longing, he rose above her, making sure their eyes locked, and plunged into her in one swift, hard motion, watching as her mouth opened in response. That mouth that had loved him and yelled at him and turned red with passion and hunger for him. He climaxed with his lips on hers, his tongue thrusting in and out of her mouth, so that he was inside of her from both ends, from everywhere, all at the same time. He wanted her to consume all of him and all of him to fill her, so that neither of them would be wanting, any existing emptiness driven out of them with force.

"Is it okay if I just lay here for a bit? Just like this? With me inside you?" He asked her, just in case, but he knew she would say yes. She always did, but Carl wanted to be a gentleman about it. It was a privilege to rest inside a woman's womb once sex had ended. He loved the warmth of her, the feeling of being enveloped and held by her insides. It was the loveliest, most fulfilling part of lovemaking for him. This part. Resting, spent and limp, inside her. For as long as he could.

When his member finally slipped out of her, unable to sustain a longer erection, he drifted away from her, kissing her on the lips again.

"Was it alright, darling?" He asked, aware of her eyes as they opened and closed in response. "I love making love to you, Camilla. You breathe life back into me. I feel like a young man again, not this broken, frail man I have become."

He saw her lips move and took it as a sign of agreement. Maybe even contentment.

"I sure hope you're happy, my love. You make me so very happy. I can't imagine my life without you. You understand?" His eyes probed hers for meaning, for understanding, and when her lids closed and opened again, resting on him with love, he was pleased.

"Let me clean you up a bit. You're bare and beautiful, and if I don't cover you up, I may have to take you again, Camilla. And I'm sure you're too exhausted for another round. I know I am." He laughed aloud, a hearty sound that filled the room and swept away some somberness that had found its home there like downy clusters of dust clinging to aged and untouched surfaces.

Carl went into the adjoining bathroom and came out with the Walgreens bag he had picked up from the pharmacist's during his weekly treks into town. He pulled out a few bottles and containers, opened them up, and brought them over to the bedside. He wiped down Camilla's body, legs, and arms with a wet towel, dried her skin, and then applied some lotions on her limbs.

"This must feel so much better," he told her, comforting her with a gentle gaze. Carl waited until her eyes met his, reassured by the gratitude he found there. He continued to apply the ointment to her legs, her toes, her fingertips, forcing the chapped hardness and dryness of her skin to succumb to the moisture wanting to find its way out. Her body glowed with hydration, and pleased with himself, Carl inhaled the scents of honey and calla lilies that enveloped the room and emanated from Camilla's clenched pores, opening them up, and letting the fragrances in.

Carl dressed her in a new nightgown he had recently purchased for her. She had gotten so small, so shriveled, that he had to buy her clothing a few sizes down from her natural size five attire. The fabric of her gown was a muted blue. Set against the pallid shade of her skin, she possessed the look of a sickly child, fading before his very eyes.

He shoved his chin into his chest so she couldn't see the wetness in his eyes as he pulled the hem of her nightdress down to her ankles, squeezed her toes with affection, and dragged the covers up to her shoulders, tucking them beneath her bony arms.

"All snug as a bug," he teased her, planting a loud, tender kiss on her lips. She had always loved his kisses, even the noisy ones he had planted on her belly button and neck. He made a ceremony of kissing her loudly just to rouse her laughter, which was like a thick palate of colors painted on his chest. That's what her laughter felt and sounded like. Colors everywhere, heavy and thick with vitality.

But she didn't laugh this time. She couldn't muster up the strength needed to laugh or yell or live out loud. She was a vanishing pale yellow, the color of rot and disease.

Carl patted her arms, thin and scrawny to his touch, and scrambled into the bathroom. He was still naked and caked with his fluids, so he took a long shower, soaping off the sweat and grime of the day as well as their lovemaking. The memories of Camilla from a long time ago, the youthfulness that had dissolved like fine sugar in a scalding teapot, the sound of her laughter chasing the hairs up his arms, leaving behind unrestrained chills, quelled only by her body writhing with yearning beneath his when he erupted violently inside her.

Drying off the pining he still harbored for the younger version of his wife, the one who responded to his touch like a wildflower with overbearing vines wanting to be tamed, crawling and winding around his limbs until he subdued her, Carl dressed slowly and made his way to the bed he shared with Camilla. He lay his weary body beside hers, turned her around carefully so she would face him, and fell asleep gazing into the reflection of himself he could only find in his Camilla.

CHAPTER 12

Camilla caressed her flat belly, exiting the doctor's office, a smile flickering along the pouty frame of her lips.

She was pregnant. This is what she wanted since the first time she kissed Carl. To give him a baby. To carry it for him. To offer him a part of her, something that would live and thrive inside her and come out resembling him. That is the poetic symmetry he looked for in the poems he taught to a group of jaded college kids who didn't notice the marvel she had found in him.

Camilla planned out the day, the way she would tell him, and detoured away from her car, heading to the supermarket instead. Wine, she thought. Lots of wine. And then she stopped short and laughed aloud. She couldn't have wine. Not for the next seven months. It was a sacrifice she was willing to make for the safety of her child. Their child.

A few hours later and a few visits to the bathroom to ease the nausea trembling up her esophagus, Camilla waited patiently in the living room for Carl to return to her from his last lecture of the day.

When he entered the foyer and placed his briefcase full of ungraded papers on the floor, she sauntered toward him with a grin even he found contagious, smiling back at her with his entire face moving in response to her charm. He received her kiss, tender against his mouth, and wordlessly followed her down the hallway, through the kitchen, and toward the backyard.

They stopped at the water bank that met their land a few hundred yards away. Camilla knew every spot in which they made love, and from the lopsided grin on his face, she knew he was thinking about the numerous times they had rolled around on the grass, naked, beneath the stars and blue skies, water rocking against their ankles and toes, as they became one, repeatedly.

This time, she led him to a blanket she had laid out beneath the grand oak, standing tall and proud a few feet away from the water bank. It was past five in the afternoon and chilly, so she was glad to have brought two extra blankets they could wrap around their bodies.

She laid down the blankets beneath the oak tree, her fingers still gripping Carl's, and watched him take in the view. The sun was drowsy against the muted sky. The tree's branches and its red-orange leaves hung low above the blanket, almost hiding the contents laid out for them.

"A picnic," he said, his stomach grumbling at the sight of food Camilla had prepared. There were cheese and crackers, olives, grapes, and bread, already buttered and wrapped in a small towel nestled in a basket. "It's lovely, Camilla. But what's the occasion?"

"Why does there need to be an occasion?" She turned to him and smacked a careless kiss on his cheek. "Come on, let's eat. I'm famished."

Carl almost tripped after her. The way she said "famished" implied more than just food. It always surprised him, the way he responded to her, the way his body melted at the sound of her voice. Would he never tire of her? Would her body and skin and sex ever become too familiar to excite him? He couldn't see that day. Everything she did and said continued to arouse him, his skin itching for her touch. His body awakened every time the sound of her voice caressed him, making love to him before she even made contact with him. He wasn't a godly man, but he prayed the feelings she birthed in him would never evaporate, never loosen their hold on him. He was enraptured. Transfixed. In love with the wisp of a girl sharing his bed and her life with him.

"It's magical," he whispered in her hair when she knelt beside him on the thick blanket separating them from the scratchy grass blades beneath them. "You're magical, and I love you so much, Camilla. I hope you feel it to your bones, how much love there is in me for you."

The moisture collecting in Carl's eyes moved Camilla, and she kissed him on the mouth, noticing the way it trembled beneath hers. She found him endearing, and the thought of holding back the gift she had for him was breaking her resolve to wait until after their bellies were full.

"I have a gift for you." She reached beneath the blanket and took out a small, thin box wrapped in pastel blue paper.

"This...you.. This is gift enough, my darling. I want for nothing more."

"You'll want this one. Trust me." She pushed the box into his hands until his own fingers took possession of it.

She watched as he tore the paper off, her eyes fixed on his features, her knees tucked beneath the weight of her body, vibrating with excitement.

When he pulled out the pale blue onesie with the words, "I love my daddy," inscribed on the cotton fabric, it took him a few seconds to respond.

"Are you...? You're...?" He stuttered, his mouth hanging open, unable to utter a full sentence to the end.

"Congratulations, Carl," Camilla murmured thickly, her eyes filling up with emotions and tears. "You're going to be a daddy."

Carl pulled the onesie to his face and wept into it, full, heavy sobs that shook his entire body.

Camilla threw herself at him and clasped her hands around his neck. The onesie bunched up between them, soaked in their tears, their joy. Carl loosened his grip on her, moved back so his eyes could look into hers.

"Thank you." He closed the space between them and kissed her in a way he hoped she had never been kissed before. His mouth, soft and open, took hers the way his body would soon take her, with abandon, with dominance, without reservations. Their kiss was deep and devouring, as if he hoped to touch and kiss the baby that was budding inside of her, growing in the lush and fertile grounds of her womb the way his flowers blossomed in his garden. He had cared for her and loved her, the way he did for his calla lilies and white roses, and now she was sowing the fruits of his endeavors, his labor, his love. There would be another Camilla among them, and he hoped for a little girl who would resemble the woman he loved more than anything or anyone in his entire life. It would be just the three of them against the entire world. He gasped inside her mouth, a thick, solid cry full of joy that left his body and entered hers through their mouths. A mating. A love like no other.

They made love on the blanket, a slow, tender montage of movements aware of the seed growing inside her, amidst the cheeses and crackers and grapes. Afterwards, Camilla lay on her bare back, Carl's head curled against her belly, his one hand cupped around her naked breast, twisting the nipple with an absent-minded compulsion. Camilla pulled ripe red grapes from the stem and popped them into her mouth, reaching down and offering Carl a few by pressing them to his lips.

"Cheese, please," he mumbled, his mouth wet against her stomach. She laughed, reached over, placed a cube of cheese on a cracker and passed it down to his lips. Camilla heard the crunch and the movement of his jaw moving up and down against her hipbones. She gasped when his fingers found solace inside her, still moist from their previous encounter. Writhing beneath him, she placed a piece of cheese lower on her belly, and then another, even lower, making a trail for him to follow with his mouth. He took one piece of cheese with his mouth, chewed it, and then lowered himself for the next, until his mouth found the bit of cheese she wanted him to end up with, resting up against her vulva. He took the cheese into his mouth and chewed, his lips moving up and down against the pulsing lips of her womanhood. Camilla writhed and moved her hips against him, wanting to feel his mouth on the hot, wet place that only he could love. She moaned when his mouth finally made direct contact and his tongue separated her lips and pressed into her. His fingers joined, pushing in and out, circling along her insides, flicking her clitoris until it puckered in response, hard and hot against the touch. When her body shuddered in response, he pulled himself up and plunged himself into her, watching her face as he moved in rhythm to her orgasm.

She grasped for his hands, and knowing what she wanted from him, he placed his fingers around her throat and squeezed ever so slightly, loosening his grip when he saw her eyes roll back into their sockets. She liked the feeling of experiencing an orgasm and darkness at the same time. He understood her. And he knew when to squeeze and when to pull back to give her the sensation she desired. It was a game of trust, and each time, she trusted him with her life. With her first and last breath. It was a gift, this trust. And he promised never to fail her.

CHAPTER 13

Camilla was kneeling in soil, collecting tomatoes from Carl's garden behind their home when a sharp pain overtook her lower abdomen. It was like a barbed wire had been shoved into her insides, twisting and grinding against the walls of her uterus. She felt a trickle of liquid slide out of her, and when she pulled her skirt up and touched the inside of her thigh with her fingertip, she found traces of blood on it.

"Carl!" She screamed. Her fingers clasped about her belly as if to contain the life that had been growing inside her. Contain and protect it, she thought as she ran through the back door leading into their kitchen.

"Carl!" Her voice was tremulous this time, and tears collected in her eyes, rolling down her cheeks as if escaping the ache contained by her body.

This is how Carl found her when he dashed down the stairs, his dusty brown and gray hair still wet from the shower. It was Sunday. They had made love in the morning and lazed about the bed until mid-day, going over a list of names Camilla had put together for the baby. He wanted a sturdy name for a boy. Henry or Thomas. She wanted something dreamy, like Antoine. If a girl, Carl told her to name the baby whatever she wanted, and Camilla sounded out names on her tongue until the one that felt natural to her lips was Gabriella. It sounded like a song, a melody that moved inside her blood as if it belonged there, its roots immersed in the foundation of her flesh.

"Carl," she sobbed. "I'm bleeding. Something's wrong. I know it." Her body sank onto the last step on the staircase beneath his feet, the frame of him thin and muscular despite his lack of working out. He took long walks in the garden, in the wall of woods behind their home, but mostly he sat and read and planned his lectures. But he never gained a pound, not an inch of fat or the pesky love handles most people his age were concerned about.

"Darling, let's take you to the hospital." He sat beside her, took her hand in his, and kissed the knuckles until they warmed and loosened.

"What if we lose this baby?" She turned her dark eyes to his with a helplessness that seemed to bolster him, made him feel as if he had more courage than he did. She seemed like a little girl just then. He wanted to comfort her, love away the fears she had developed like overgrown weeds he couldn't control without destroying the rest of her. The healthy parts of her.

"We don't know anything like that will happen. Let's go get a sonogram and see what's happening. Women bleed all the time while pregnant and they still give birth to healthy, beautiful children."

Wiping a tear from her cheek, she turned her body to him. "How do you know this?" Eyebrows arched high across her forehead, she tossed him a doubtful look, one that said she knew he was making things up to pacify her.

"I've been doing some reading." Catching another dubious expression on her features, he laughed aloud. "You're not the only one reading *What to Expect When You're Expecting*, you know. I have my own copy."

Camilla's laugh was weak in response, her body hardly shaking by the movement needed to dispense a natural one.

"Let me put a shirt on. Grab your coat, and I'll get the car. It will all be fine. You'll see. Come on. Let's go get some answers." He patted her knee, rose from his place beside her, and trekked up the stairs in search of a shirt that would cover the thin layer of white hairs on his chest.

The drive to the hospital was a quiet one, both lost in their own thoughts, their own worries, their fingers intertwined for unspoken support and camaraderie as they drove down the street littered with cherry blossoms ripped from branches of the trees by the force of the autumn winds. Camilla watched them collide and collect on the windshield in front of her, and she sensed doom wrap his arms around her shoulders, darkness overcoming her.

"Camilla." She heard Carl's voice from a distance, dragging her into the present. He was shaking her, and the force of being pulled and pushed by his frantic hands brought her back to him, her eyes opening to search his concerned ones.

"Where did you go?" He asked her.

She let out a laugh that came out empty and fractured, almost tearing at the flesh of his fingers, still wrapped around her arms. He let go.

"I guess I just fell asleep," she muttered, but he didn't hear her. He was out of the car already, moving to her side and opening the door for her to get out. He took on her weight with his own crumpled shoulders, fearing more the weight of things they didn't know yet. Death. Loss. He tried not to gasp at the blood she left behind when she rose from the passenger side of his gray Toyota.

An officer by the ER door noticed them and met them by the curb of the street with a wheelchair, helping Carl place her gently into it. An older nurse from behind the check-in counter took one look at their pallid expressions and came around to the front.

"Let's get you into a room, darling." Within minutes, Camilla was in a bed, lying prostrate in a row of many beds with only a blue curtain separating them, and hooked to an IV line while waiting for the doctor to see them. A nurse performed a transvaginal ultrasound, placing a thin and gel-swabbed wand inside of her and moving it around while snapping at the keys to sharpen, widen, and still the images of her uterus. She did this quietly, her eyes masked.

Camilla's heart was so loud and thick in her ears, she wondered if the rest of the women in her room could also hear it. She caught sight of Carl's pulse on his neck, and it beat in rhythm to her own heart, fast and heavy throbbing that seemed to push up against the surface of skin for just one breath. They were suffocating under the weight of all the unknowns that raced ahead of them, and they were trying to catch up, to slow the moment down, to end the impending doom of this one day.

"Just get it over with," Camilla snapped at her doctor when she strolled into her cubicle and pulled the curtain closed behind her. Her doctor eyed the machine and the results without emotion and placed her eyes on Camilla's face with such gentleness that Camilla almost felt the soft caress on her cheek.

"I'm sorry, Camilla. There's no fetal heartbeat and your HCG levels have decreased." Dr. Moran paused.

"Which means?" Camilla prodded her. "You have to say it." Her voice was hard and calm. She already knew, but she had to hear the words. Her body had to hear them and sink into them so there would be no parts of her still waiting for hope. She wanted Carl to hear the words also, so she wouldn't have to pass them on to him, to watch the disappointment swim in his eyes and bury itself on his cheeks and chin. Maybe if the doctor told him, then they wouldn't have to speak of this ever again.

"You've lost the baby. You're miscarrying, and because of the amount of blood you're shedding, we can't do a D&C. It's already progressed, so your body has to expel the fetus on its own. You can do it here, or you can go home. It's a very natural process and very common."

"I want to go home." The doctor nodded and stepped back from the bed. "I'll get the discharge papers. Call me if you need anything."

The nurse wiped the gel from her vagina and handed her the clothing she had come to the hospital with, still caked with blood.

The ride back home was quiet. There was nothing to say. Nothing to save. It was all done. Finished.

That night, Camilla found herself on the bathroom floor, in agony, as the fetus inside her expelled itself. She sat on the toilet bowl while her insides spasmed and gushed out of her, weeping into her hands, screaming in pain. Her body was going through the motions of giving birth, except nothing but death was coming out of her. When it all seemed to be over, Camilla knelt on her knees and looked into the bloodbath that remained in the bowl. She slipped her hands into the red grave water and pulled out the remains of a baby that had not wanted to grow inside of her. Maybe it knew who she was, deep down, and rejected her for it. Why wouldn't this baby want to be born to her? Unless it had already known that she would be a failure. A bad mother.

She laid the clotted and gelatinous bits of herself, of her baby-that-did-not-want-to-be, on the floor in a straight line and fingered them, trying to find the face, the belly, the feet. Any signs of human form she could make out of the blobs of blood and matter that no longer lived and breathed inside her. There was nothing. She couldn't make any sense of them, just as she couldn't make any sense of her miscarriage, of how swiftly happiness could be erased from one's life. From her life.

"What are you doing?" Carl's voice shook her from her stupor, and his arms reached out to pull her up and away from the bloody carcass that lay by her feet, her fingers trying to untangle the mass of blood and guts, shape it into a baby she could fold into her arms and sing to sleep.

Camilla pushed his hands away from her. "Leave me alone, Carl."

Carl tucked his hands into his corduroy pockets and hung his chin low on his chest. "You're acting crazy, Camilla. Stop this."

He stood there for a while, willing her to look at him, to find solace in him as she had in the past, but she kept fingering the remains, shaking her head, blood sticking to her fingers and nightgown and legs. He went downstairs, unable to watch her anymore, and as soon as his feet hit the lower step on the staircase, he fell to his knees and stifled the lone sob that rushed from his lungs and into his throat like a raging river.

His Camilla was fading. He had watched the light in her extinguish on the car ride from the hospital to their home, and when she climbed the stairs to disappear into their room, under the covers of their bed, the light had been smothered. What remained in the girl he loved was only a darkness he didn't have the will to contain.

CHAPTER 14

Carl spent the next few weeks moving around like an automaton. His legs dragged him from his home to his lectures and then back to his home again. He rattled off his poetry in a monotone voice that made his students fall asleep or disappear from his courses. But he didn't care. He didn't care about his job, his poets, or his students. Not anymore. The only person he cared about was Camilla, who had locked herself in the painting room he had designed and decorated for her. Away from him. From his eyes and hands and love. He hadn't touched her since the miscarriage, his hands itching with the desire to slide over her pale, bare skin when she was asleep. While the urge was there, he couldn't do it. He knew deep down that touching her now, after this irreparable loss, would cost him all of Camilla. And although he missed loving her, hearing her laughter, the sounds of her moving beneath him while in the throes of passion, he dared not touch her. She had replaced her skin with metal armor and had built walls around her to keep them apart.

"I don't understand you," he told her one night when he felt her crawl into bed at three in the morning.

She was silent.

He continued, knowing she could hear him. "We both lost something here. Both of us. But we should lean on each other, not add more distance."

More silence.

"I love you, Camilla. I only want to take your pain away. Or to feel the pain with you. Let me."

A sigh this time, barely audible, made it to his ears.

"Just give me time, Carl. I just need some time."

It was not the answer Carl wanted, but he relented just the same. He rolled to the edge of his bed and stared into darkness, wishing he could erase the past few weeks, the pain, the loss, the baby that had come like an easy breeze but left behind a storm neither one of them had expected or been prepared for. Carl listened for the cadence in her breathing and found his own breaths matching hers. He wanted them to be one, fall asleep as one, even though their backs were to each other, the fortified but invisible line she had drawn keeping them apart.

When he woke in the morning, her place on the bed was unoccupied and cold. On his way to the bathroom, he put his ear to the door of her drawing room, listening for sounds of her. He heard faint movements and released a sigh of relief. Each morning, when he opened his eyes and found her missing from their bed, he half-expected that she'd be gone. Left him. He was relieved when he found her holed up in her room, painting, or whatever it was she was doing in there.

He hadn't known this side of her. She had never shown him her dark places. Had never spoken of them. So, he assumed they hadn't existed. But he should have known better. Everyone has dark and jagged edges. He had been a fool to only look at the light in her and expect there to be no underbelly. She had seduced him with her body, the dark eyes that seemed to lick him like a cat every time she placed them on him. Anger boiled up inside of him for the first time.

No, he shook his head at himself. She was suffering. Everyone suffers differently. Give her time, he told himself. Give her space.

"Camilla will come back to me," he whispered to the breeze that caught his silver hair and pulled it away from his forehead as he made his way out of the house and stood at the top of the teal steps she had painted out of boredom. The same steps they had made love upon countless times, her body riding his, her legs circling his waist, her hair falling in his eyes as she moaned into his mouth.

Lines creased the skin around his eyes, and he drew them to the sun inching her way from behind a series of clouds, trying to come out, to face him, to fill him with the heat and energy he needed to get through the day. Another day without Camilla smiling at him and touching him. Her absence made his skin prickle with agitation. Walking to his car, he raised his arms to invite some warmth from the sun's rays angling toward him, and when heat touched his skin, a chill of surprise overtook him. He spun, his eyes glimpsing Camilla staring at him from the bedroom window on the second floor. He gave her a slight wave. She didn't wave back, only retreated behind the curtains without so much as a smile, a nod, a flicker of awareness. Nothing.

Stepping on the gas and pulling out of their long driveway, leaving a trail of dust behind him, Carl wondered where this side of Camilla had been all this time. Why had she surfaced only now, well into their marriage, his love for her, so that he had no way of ever expecting it? He felt cheated, lied to.

He didn't want this Camilla. She was not the woman he had desired and loved and made a home with. She was not what she had promised, what she had led him to believe, and he couldn't help but feel deceived. Tricked, somehow. Bitterness coursed through his bloodstream like an invisible worm consuming him from the inside.

CHAPTER 15

Camilla's heavy sigh awakened her. Blinking until her eyes found comfort in the darkness, she listened for Carl's presence, afraid this would be the day that he would leave her. After all, why wouldn't he? She couldn't give him a baby. Her insides were cold and dark and barren of life. How could he want her now?

She inhaled deeply when she realized he was not in the bed beside her, where he often was at four in the morning. Camilla often watched him sleep, sometimes moving a loose thread of gray hair from his forehead. She could only touch him at night, when he slept, afraid to touch him when he might respond to her, wanting to love her. She felt unlovable, covered in a blanket of frost and bitterness that wanted no softness, no love to bear it down. Camilla wanted something else. To be struck. To feel pain or something other than this numbing emptiness inside her.

Camilla pushed her legs over the mattress and realized she had slept in her clothes from the day before. She had done that often these past few weeks. How long had it been? Four? Five weeks? Pushing her dark hair from her face, she walked out of the room to find Carl.

"Carl?" She called out, surprised by the husky tremble in her voice. She had not spoken in all this time. Had not heard her own voice, had forgotten what it sounded like, what it felt like to say words aloud, to speak to someone other than the demons living inside her, telling her how worthless she was, how vacant and vile.

Moving quietly down the hallway, her ears pricked at the sound of papers being shuffled. It came from her drawing room. She thought she had locked it. She didn't want Carl in there. To see what she had done. What she had created when words had ceased to be available to her.

Pushing the door open, she blinked hard in the dark until her eyes found him. He was sitting on the floor, hunched over a pile of her canvases drawn out before him like a deck of cards. He looked so alone, sitting there, his back rounded and caved in as if he were bearing the weight of the world on his spine. Guilt over causing this portrait of dejection pushed down the anger, the violation she felt over finding him among her things, her drawings, her pain. She wanted to touch him, to soothe away the hurt she had poured into him without his consent, without asking if he could sustain it and not flinch or break under its force.

"Carl?" He didn't answer.

She moved closer to his bent back, stood over him, afraid to find what he had been looking at. She was right. The six canvases stretched out before him were covered in red, the color of rage and blood and loss. The night she had miscarried, she had laid out the bits and pieces of her insides, the baby that didn't want to be, and had memorized each red and purple mass before placing it gently back into the toilet and flushing it as if it were a dead pet fish or one's own excrement. She painted each one of those images, the fragments of mass and flesh and death, bloodied and severed from her uterus. Six paintings for six fragments of a fetus torn to bits on its way out of the warm cocoon she had built for it. A natural abortion, a self-imposed suicide that had left her insides raw, rendering her gasping for air, for relief from the pain of pushing out a baby that she was desirous of keeping in, protecting, growing until it was ready for its first breath outside of her womb.

"What is this?" Carl hissed suddenly, his back still to her.

"It's our baby." And then she watched as the muscles on his back quaked, broken sobs running out of his mouth as if trying to escape the pain that had found root in him and clung on like a bed of interminable vines climbing the walls of an unkempt home.

Camilla fell on her knees and wrapped her arms around Carl from behind, locking him to her chest, her own body shaking, her own mouth full of sobs she had kept down like regurgitated bile for the last month since she had lost their baby.

"I'm so sorry, Carl. I'm so, so sorry I couldn't give you a baby." The words came out in a growl, wet with tears, and rested in the folds of his neck. She leaned her head against the hard expanse of his back, soothed by the steady rhythm of his breathing, until her cries dissipated. She felt him moving beneath her head and touch, and before she knew it, he was facing her, his arms snaking around her and pulling her hard against his chest.

"Don't leave me again, Camilla. I don't think I can take it. Not again."

"I didn't leave you, Carl." His words surprised her, and Camilla inched her head and chest away from his to look into his eyes. They were moist and dark gray, and she could see the loneliness and sadness seated side by side in them, like two old men, hunched and broken, forgotten by life and love all together with only the other to keep him company.

"You did," he accused her. "You were here, but you weren't. It was like living with a ghost, Camilla. I thought I lost you."

"I'm sorry, Carl. I wasn't thinking, really. I just felt all this pain, all this guilt, and I didn't want to see disappointment in your eyes. Not when they look at me. I don't think I could bear it if you hated me, were disappointed in me."

"Disappointed? Why would I be disappointed in you?" Carl, still on his knees, leaned back into them to get a better look at her. How he had missed her. Had missed her voice and the way the sounds of her words trickled all over him like cool water on a hot day. He felt refreshed and renewed, and he wanted to swallow this moment before it disappeared again.

"Because I couldn't give you a baby. Because my body is not good enough, not strong enough to have one." Her voice cracked and broke, her head sinking into his chest as another bout of sobs overtook her.

"Now, now," Carl soothed her, kissing the top of her hair, inhaling the scent of her lavender conditioner, his arms holding her against him as if he was the shelter she needed. "I am disappointed that you disappeared in your grief, Camilla, but not because you had a miscarriage. Miscarriages are common. It doesn't mean you're not strong or a woman if you have one. But you can't disappear like that again, Camilla. I won't have it. I'm your husband. And I lost the baby, too. We need to grieve together, not apart. We should be leaning on each other. You're all I have. All I need in this life. Do you understand me?"

He pushed the tangled strands of hair away from her wet face and looked at her until she pulled her eyes to his like two lovers bumping into each other after a long absence.

"I understand, Carl. I love you, too." She smiled at him and reached over to plant a tentative kiss on his mouth. He tasted like grief, his lips stained with salt and wetness from the tears he had shed. Hunger rolled in her insides like an untamed animal that had tasted blood and wanted more. She deepened her kiss until she felt him respond, his own mouth opening beneath the force of hers, hot and ravenous, while her tongue snaked into his for a deeper taste.

"Carl," she said thickly into his mouth. "Take me to bed."

CHAPTER 16

Carl and Camilla spent the next six months crawling back into the folds of their wooly cocoon again, a slow process weighted with the grief that comes hand-in-hand with a loss no one truly understands or can assign words to. They struggled to find those words, weeping into each other now instead of empty rooms and hollow pillows designed to mute out sounds of agony and betrayal.

They talked into the darkness, holding hands, and they made love with a voracious hunger that made up for several weeks spent walking about each other as if untethered ghosts who couldn't find their way back to the light. To love.

"Carl," Camilla whispered to him one night as they settled into bed and she had just turned off the light.

"Hmm," he nuzzled his nose into her neck, inhaling the smells of her that aroused his senses, blinding him almost, his hands already reaching out for the parts of her that would house his.

"I think I'm pregnant."

There was a pause. A long one that neither of them knew how to fill with words. Or which words they should let spill into the space between them without the other falling apart, growing distant again, shaking with fear at what all these unfamiliar words meant.

"Are you sure?" He asked, his hands suspended above her breasts, his lips grasping bits of hair as he pulled his mouth away from her skin.

"Mmm, yes. My breasts are raw, I missed my period, and I'm getting those nauseating sensations in the back of my throat. Like I need to throw up."

There was a pause. "And I took a pregnancy test earlier today. It was positive."

"Why didn't you tell me?"

"I've had a feeling, but I wanted to be sure before I told you. I didn't want to hurt you again. I still don't. What if this pregnancy doesn't make it either? I'm so afraid, Carl." Camilla stifled the fear rising in her throat. She wouldn't lose it this time, she promised herself. Her body trembled with the effort it took to control her emotions, her anxiety.

"There's nothing to be afraid of, Camilla. This is wonderful news. It will be okay. Whatever happens. Because we have each other, and we've been through this already. We know what to expect, what signs to look for. We know how to handle it."

"I'm afraid to lose you, Carl."

"You won't. I promise. We're in this together. A team. I won't go anywhere. Promise me you won't either."

"I promise, Carl. I'll try."

Camilla reached for his hand and pulled it to her mouth, kissing the smooth, hard knuckles she had spent so much of the time watching. His hands were beautiful, strong, lovely to look at, and her eyes were transfixed by them when he did simple things like pour tea or read one of his books or pass them all over her body as if they were looking for meaning there, answers that his books and poems and dead poets didn't offer him.

"Carl," she began, her voice so small that Carl inched closer to her in the dark to hear her.

"Yes, darling."

"I have to tell you something. Something I'm afraid you won't like."

A long pause ensued, followed by the sounds of their breathing in the dark. They were both shaking with uncertainty, afraid of the words that trembled to come out from the place where secrets lived inside her, dark and lonely and unuttered.

"What is it?" He coaxed, impatient with the waiting of any bad news.

"Promise you won't hate me first."

"Camilla, I'm your husband. There's nothing you can tell me that will make me hate you. Can't you feel how much I love you?"

"Yes, I can. But this... this can change all of that."

Another pause was full of the heavy breathing of their fears. Carl could feel his heart pulsing beneath the skin of his nightshirt as thoughts of her rolling around with other men surfaced in his mind's eye.

"You cheated on me." This was not a question.

Camilla sat up and shifted to face him. He saw the white of her eyes reflected in the moonlight that snuck through the windowpanes of their room.

"God, no! Carl! I would never!"

He heaved a sigh of relief and tried to manage his breaths to slow down the rapid thumping of his heart.

"Do you think that low of me?" Camilla hissed in the dark.

"You said I would hate you if you told me this thing, and this is the only thing I could imagine hating you for, Camilla. Give me a break. Just tell me already. You're killing me." He sat up and faced her, their eyes clashing in the dimly lit room.

"I had an abortion. Two actually."

"Oh." He nodded, relieved her confession had not been about her cheating with other men. "Is that all?"

"You're not angry? Disappointed?"

"Of course not. I know you, Camilla. If you had an abortion..."

"Two abortions," she corrected.

He smiled. "If you had two abortions, it's because you had to. Do you want to tell me about them?"

"Well," she began, her voice quiet, her breath fanning against his cheekbone as the words came out in a stream of confessions uttered for the first time. "The first time, I was fifteen. He was older, a man, a friend of my father's. He was always at the house with his wife, so I'd known him all my life. I constantly found his eyes on me, but I didn't mind. I liked the way he watched me. It made me feel good, desired. So, when he came into my room one night when my dad had a few guys over for poker, I thought nothing of it. He wasn't my first, or my fourth, really. It was nice to have a man touching me instead of the boys I'd known my age. It always felt like they were practicing on me, awkward and stiff. But Jeff, the man, he knew what he was doing. He had practiced on others and used what he had learned on me, and it felt wonderful to be loved by him."

She took a deep breath, and Carl waited, his fingers gently sliding over her trembling hands.

"I think I loved him, too. We saw each other here and there. He booked hotel rooms for us and we made love during his lunch break. Twice in his house, on his bed, when his wife was out of town. But when I told him I was pregnant, it was all over. He paid for my abortion and that was it. I called him a few times, but he found reasons not to call back or to get off the phone quickly. He just faded out of my life, you see. He even stopped hanging out with my dad. I never saw him again after that."

"Did he go with you, for the abortion?" Carl asked.

"He was supposed to. He said he'd be there. But then he called me at the last minute, while I was in the waiting room of the clinic, and told me he had a last-minute meeting he couldn't miss. So, I went in by myself. I cried the entire time. I never felt so alone in all my fifteen years. I slept for days afterward, and I didn't get out of the slump until my father threatened to take me to a psychiatrist. That did it for sure," she laughed, tears trickling into her mouth.

"And the second time?" Carl prodded after a moment of silence.

"I was nineteen. A freshman in college. I don't remember much of it. I had gone to a fraternity party with a few of my friends. I drank a lot in those days, you know, for fun. But then I blacked out and woke up the next morning in an empty room at the fraternity house. I wasn't the only one. You should have seen us, a string of girls gaining consciousness, half-naked, bleary-eyed, trying to figure out what had happened the night before, searching everywhere for our missing panties. My insides were raw and caked with a sticky substance, and it was obvious I had had sex, but I couldn't remember any of it. Not even the guy. A few months later, I'm running out of my Economics class and throwing up in the hallway. It was a mess."

"Did anyone go with you this time? To the clinic?" Carl asked, shaken by the idea of men taking advantage of her, her body, without her knowledge or wherewithal.

"No. But it was fine. The nurse held my hand the whole time. She was very maternal, really. She spoke to me during the entire process, telling me everything would be okay. I believed her, you know? And it was, eventually."

Carl nodded, unsure of what to say to Camilla, to ease the frown lines that had found some permanence on her forehead. But he had no words. Only anger. For the men that had used her up. For the loneliness she had suffered. The guilt of aborting pregnancies on her own, no one there to support her, love her through the bad and the good.

"It's almost ironic now," she continued, her voice reaching out to him, sliding around his shoulders, intertwining with the hair on his chest, almost pulling him to her.

"What is?" His voice was soft, to match the somber lull in hers.

"That I had a miscarriage. It's like I'm being punished for having not one but two abortions. Because I wasn't careful or ready. But now I'm ready, Carl. I want our baby to be brought into this life through me, through my body. But what if it's too damaged? Too used up. Too corrupted by my carelessness. What if I lose this one, too?" Her voice broke again, and her head fell against the wall of his chest, trembling with sobs.

"Camilla, you're not being punished. You're a lovely human being who found herself in precarious spots without guidance or help. You're good, my darling. Having an abortion doesn't take away who you are. Your worth. There's no one out there keeping count and doling out justice, you know. Just you. So, stop it."

He placed both hands on either side of her head and pulled her off his chest so he could capture her eyes with his. Gently. Lovingly. As if she were a brand-new baby whose head needed to be secured and handled with care. That's how he saw her in this moment. Vulnerable. In need of care and love, both of which had been absent from her life.

"I love you. Nothing will change that. Nothing you say or do will rob you of my feelings for you. Do you understand?"

She nodded, smoothing her free hand across her runny nose. She forced a smile at him, wanting to trust him. "I believe you," she said, not giving voice to the doubts that lived in her bones. Her father had said similar words to her a long time ago. But when he found out about the first abortion, when she was fifteen and a nurse from the clinic called her home to see if she had recovered well, her father had screamed. And he had never screamed in all the years he had raised her. She had only known him as a lonely, brooding man. Especially after her mother had died. But he had berated her, called her a whore, and stormed out of the house, into his car, to the nearest bar he could find.

He had returned drunk that night. Woke her up when he sat on the edge of her bed. She could smell the beer on him, in the dark.

"I forgive you, Camilla. Let's never talk about this again."

"Like it never happened?" She asked as she felt him move away from her in the dark and toward the door.

"Like it never happened." He closed the door behind him, locking her in the dark, and she cried herself to sleep. Things between them were different from that point forward. It's as if he had built a wall between them overnight. They ate dinner silently. They passed each other in the kitchen or in the hallway on their way to their respective rooms without looking at each other, without any words between them. It didn't feel like "it" had never happened. It felt more like he was punishing her. Like he hadn't forgiven her.

Camilla sometimes found him looking at her, his eyes pressed against her face, in search of answers she didn't know the questions to. He opened his mouth as if to say something, but then shut it again after he shoved a spoonful of soup or a chunk of chicken into it, stuffing his words back down. She said nothing, mainly out of fear. What if he asked who the father had been? What would she say? *Your best friend. The man who has known me since I was seven.*

She couldn't reveal Jeff's identity. Not to her father. He would never understand. He would hate her, especially since Jeff had ceased to exist in their lives. He had bowed out of poker game after poker game until her father had stopped asking him. Jeff had not contacted her since the day before her abortion, stuffing the cash into her fingers and walking away from her, saying he would be there, if he could, but not showing up. Ignoring her calls. Her invitations to see her, make love to her again. Camilla would have gone back to him. She was fifteen, and he was the only warmth she had known. She thought he had loved her. He told her he did, the words flowing out of his mouth like a stream of uncontained water, his body crashing into hers, filling her with love and desire. And then nothing. Emptiness. She shivered at the memory of him, at her thin naked limbs trembling with the want of him.

Her father was supposed to love her, too. But she didn't feel love when he shut her out, thrusting her into cold corners without affection, hardly speaking to her until her eighteenth birthday. He bought her a used Honda and waved her off as she drove to Barnard for her first year of college. It's as if since the day he had found out about her abortion, he had just been waiting for her to leave his house, to leave him, before he could breathe again.

The last time Camilla saw him was when she returned home for his funeral, lying in a coffin. His features were pale and pasty, peaceful even. She had almost forgotten what he looked like. But she felt nothing as her eyes ran over his face, the thick, calloused hands that had ceased to touch her hair or place affectionate pats along her shoulders and back. The abortion had made her untouchable. Unlovable. At the first sight of her imperfections, he had withdrawn his love from her as if it were a tangible object that could be given and just as easily taken away.

And now, Carl was saying beautiful things to her, lovely things, words that promised to love her forever, despite not one but two abortions. And a miscarriage that had almost burned down the home they lived in with its wrath.

The touch of Carl's fingers on her belly brought her back to him, back to their bed, her eyes having adjusted to the darkness.

"You look like an angel," Carl whispered into her hair.

"I'm not an angel, Carl. I'm just me. Camilla."

"You're my angel. Perfect and lovely. Come, let's go to bed. It's late." He lay down and faced her, waiting for her to do the same. She relented, lay back down on the spongy mattress and turned her body and head toward him. He took her hand and placed it on his chest. Smiling, she took his and placed it on her chest. And they fell asleep like that, facing each other, placid expressions sketched on their faces, to the slow beating of each other's heart.

CHAPTER 17

The next miscarriage arrived in the middle of the night, a grinding pain surging inside Camilla that awakened her and forced her to double over. She stumbled to the bathroom and gave birth to another fetus, already dead and bloodied, as her body washed it out of her system. Unwanted. Undesirable scraps of baby that made little sense to the untrained eye.

"Camilla!" Carl rushed to her side.

"Get out!" She screamed at him, sobbing, gasping for air as each surge of pain forced her to arch her back until she thought her spine would splinter and snap in two. "Get out! Get out!" She yelled again until Carl left the bathroom and shut the door behind him. He sat on the edge of the bed they had made love in earlier that night, unaware that loss would strike at them again. He placed his head in his hands, uncomfortable with waiting while she grunted in pain and loss between her legs behind the closed door.

Why does she keep leaving me out? He thought to himself. *It's my baby, too. My loss.* He shook his head, waiting for her on the other side of the wall she had built once again between them. They hadn't named this baby yet, hadn't sat around talking about what to name him or her. They had made no plans, just in case. But he had cherished the idea of a third member of the family joining them. Had wanted a little boy or girl to run through the house asking for ice cream or to go to the park. Sometimes, it was lonely in this house with just Camilla. He loved her, more than he had loved anything or anyone in his entire life, but he knew there had to be something more than just the two of them. More than just the sex they had day in and day out, her body already an overtaken path on a trail he had pursued daily. He ached for a fresh path, something more than just her skin and body and sex. A child's bustle and laughter would have been that new path. For both of them.

He sighed with a resigned understanding that a baby would not be coming to them anytime soon. This was her second miscarriage. He didn't think she would have an appetite to try again. He didn't know if he had the appetite to try again, to feel this kind of emptiness that felt like his organs were being ripped out from his chest. To feel the fullness, happiness that comes with the idea of a child and then to have it replaced with emptiness was not something he wanted to experience again. He didn't think Camilla would either.

In the bathroom, Camilla gripped the wall to keep her steady as more blood and fragments of baby escaped her battered, worthless womb. A womb that couldn't grow a seed of happiness she needed to keep going. She was tired. Tired of gaining and losing. Why not just gain? What was the point of loss, anyway?

She didn't go to the doctor this time. Or the hospital. There was no need. Her body naturally vacated the remains of a baby that did not want to grow inside of her or have her as a mother. Why would it? She knew nothing about being a mother or raising a child. All she knew was how to please men, to lie beneath them and take them into her as if they had belonged there, had come from inside of her. She always felt that when men had sex with her, they just wanted a body, one that had resembled the woman who had given birth to them. By entering her, they were just trying to find their way back to the womb that had once kept them warm and safe.

But her womb was broken. She had destroyed it with two abortions and gratuitous sex with men of all shapes and sizes since she was thirteen and trying to find someone to fill the yawing emptiness that took up so much of her insides. She felt full for the few seconds they remained inside her, but once they pulled out, the emptiness returned, aching and burning with needs she didn't know how to satisfy.

Now not even a baby wanted to find succor in her. Was it so bad to be inside her? To live in her womb? Was it too cold or too scarred, too wasted? Was there nothing she could do to repair the damage, to take back the years of abuse and misuse she had stretched her legs wide open for, letting one stranger after another ride her like a train that made no stops, passengers jumping on and off without so much as a ticket or a thank you while she lay on her back and pretended to like it? That this was what she wanted, too?

When the last wave of agonizing pain passed through her and Camilla was sure there was nothing more to expel from her uterus, she wiped the entrails from her body with toilet paper and sank to the floor. She didn't put her arm inside the toilet bowl this time. Didn't pick out the bits of her baby that did not match any other bits. She didn't lay them out on the floor and try to make sense of them, figure how they fit into each other, where the arm or the belly would be. There was no puzzle to piece together. Only death. Loss. She didn't attempt to make sense of it this time.

Camilla pushed the lever down and flushed the baby bits into the sewer system, watching as the lumps swished in circles of blood-water until they all disappeared. A heavy sigh escaped her guarded mouth, and a shiver passed along her spine, forcing her to stand up into a straight, long line. She changed her underwear, rummaged through the hamper for the sweatpants and shirt she had worn the previous day, and opened the door.

"I don't want to talk about it, Carl." She didn't look at him as she went to her side of the bed, opened the window to let the cool air in, and buried herself beneath the covers. She curled into a fetal ball, her back to the man left to suffer this loss alone.

"Do you want me to take you to the hospital?" He asked, his voice soft, almost a murmur.

"No." Her response was clipped. "I don't want to talk. Period."

Carl bowed his head so that his chin touched his chest, took a deep breath, and crawled beneath the covers. He faced her though, his gray eyes fixed on her bent spine so when she woke up Camilla would see she wasn't alone. He would always be there. Whether or not she asked him to. He had nowhere to go, and she was his everything.

They both fell asleep, out of exhaustion, and in the morning, they woke up and went about the business of moving on. The business of forgetting.

CHAPTER 18

"Camilla." Carl knocked on her studio door, his knuckles barely touching its surface. He didn't try opening the door. He already knew it would be locked. She was back, the ghost of the woman he had married and loved with the real Camilla nowhere in sight. She hid in her studio all day, before he awoke, and didn't come out of it until he had already fallen asleep. He went to bed alone and woke up alone.

"I put some toast and coffee here for you. Please eat something." He waited for some signs of life. A word. A movement. But nothing. Pressing his ear to the door, he heard her moving about the room, and reassured that she hadn't disappeared from his life altogether, he left for work.

The drive was tedious, but everything had felt this way for Carl. Having an absent Camilla in his life was like living all of it in slow motion. Dull and bland. He didn't even notice the red and yellow leaves of the maple trees on his way to campus. He used to love slowing the car down just to prolong the line of colors that made his insides spring to life, but now, all of them seemed ordinary. His eyes didn't even search for them, staring straight ahead, the narrow road seeming endless before him.

He didn't teach today, but he went to the office, anyway. He worked every day, ever since the night Camilla had lost their baby. Lost it. He snickered at that. The phrase was ridiculous and sounded like she had misplaced it, put it somewhere they couldn't find it. It wasn't lost; it was gone. It had disappeared, just like the last one. As if it were nothing and they had to move on as if they had lost nothing precious or valuable. And they had moved on. Separately. Camilla lived in her studio, the one he had made for her so they could share her passion, her art. But she used it as a shield, locking him out of the room, her dark creations, and her heart. He hadn't even heard her voice since the night of her last miscarriage, when she had turned to him in the middle of the night and mouthed, "I'm sorry, Carl. I'm so, so sorry."

She had her studio, and he had his office. It was musty and smelled of old books and stale air. He used to love this office. It always reminded him of the first day Camilla had sauntered into it and into his life, taken him in her arms and kissed him. She had been so confident then. Audacious, seductive. It seemed so long ago, but it was in this exact office, this exact spot that she had told him she was not a child. Not the fragile Isabella of his youth. That she would not crack and break. And he had believed her. Believed in the fantasy of having a whole woman to love, who knew who she was and what she wanted. Who wouldn't disappear in empty rooms and crowded thoughts that shut him out.

He was untethered now. There seemed to be nothing, no string, holding him to her. He hated this feeling. Hated being alone, unoccupied. A part of him wished Camilla had never come into his life. She had given him everything he had abstained from—sex, love, hope— and then taken all of them away with a simple snap of her fingers. There had been no evidence to foretell how she would react to pain, suffering, and so he felt blindsided now. The way she had disappeared into herself, leaving him out in the cold. Locking doors belonging to his home, doors that had never remained closed to him before. She was changing all the rules and had not even consulted him. This was their life, after all. Not just hers. Their baby. Their home. And she had cast him out of all of it. Without a warning.

He lay on the brown leather couch in his office and placed his arm over his forehead and eyes, hoping sleep would overtake him. He was so tired. Instead, his memories traced Camilla's outline, the way she smiled at him right before she wanted to make love, the way her back arched, right on this couch, her skin sticking to its surface, all the times she had surprised him with nothing more than a coat and long boots, nakedness beneath it. Everything brought her back to him when all he wanted was a few minutes without remembering her, remembering the way she felt in his hands, soft and desirable, willing and supple. Now she was like a broken vase with jagged edges that could slice his skin if he dared touch her.

When he finally fell asleep, Carl dreamt of falling into a pit of broken glass, shards piercing his arms and legs and eyes, blinding him. He woke up screaming, his fingers grabbing at his legs and arms, trying to pull out fragments of glass protruding from his body. But there was nothing there. He shook off the sluggishness of his sleep, snatched his worn briefcase, and trudged back to his car.

Pulling into the driveway almost an hour later, he found Camilla's car was gone. She had gone out. But where? They didn't have any friends in the area. It had just been the two of them all these years. Carl scratched his head and made his way into the house that had belonged to his parents. The house that had raised him and expected nothing more from him but quiet respect.

Without thinking, he jogged up the stairs and tried the handle of Camilla's studio door. It gave in and he pushed it open, entering the room that encapsulated his wife's pain and all the other parts of her she had sheltered, pouring them only into her paintings. And there they were. All her secrets, her longings, her betrayals.

She had placed them all in plain sight for him to find. It's as if she planted them there for him, to hurt him, to show him the dark places in her he had not known about. Perhaps he had never asked about. But they were all there. Every single one of them sketched in black pencil against a series of white backgrounds. She was at the center of all of them, naked, open, her face ringed with pain and self-loathing, men prying her apart with their hands and thighs, their bare buttocks tense with ferocity. There was one in the bathroom stall of a bar, while a faceless man took her from behind, one hand squeezing her breast, his other free hand smashing her head against the graffitied wall, tears visible as they slid down her cheeks. Another of her in a car, in a dark alley, in someone's apartment, the looming shadow of a man, sometimes two men, crouched over her body, naked and limp, her face averted in pain, vacant eyes staring at him, at Carl, as if she were coming out of the paintings to say, "See, Carl. This is who you love." As if to say, "I am nothing."

Tears stung his eyes, repulsed by the images of his wife, her body naked and occupied by men whose faces remained faded and blank against the dark canvas of her paintings, taking her without seeing her. At the same time, he understood the pain scratching at her insides, understood the worthlessness she felt that made her seek sex with strangers who used her, the woman he loved, as if she didn't exist inside her body.

Carl peeled his eyes away from the portraits of self-loathing she had drawn for him, to let him know she felt numb inside, dead. He waited for anger to unfold like a brushfire in him, but nothing came. No rage, no need to lash out and break lamps or plunge a pair of scissors into the eyes staring back at him from the canvasses of her paintings. Even her betrayals in having sex with these men while he was at work did not strike him with revulsion. He only felt longing for Camilla, a deep abiding need to comfort her, to pacify and lull the anger that drove her away from him and into the arms of men who made her hate herself and her body even more.

He reached out and stroked a single tear that dropped like a diamond from her still eye, murky and cavernous against her pale skin on the canvas. He loved her still, perhaps even deeper, loss having shaped a more complicated Camilla than he had known to be possible. She was a woman now. A woman with layers in her pain vault, her eyes glassy with longing and ache intermingled, and he found her even more desirable than he had expected.

Taking a deep breath, Carl exited the studio and closed the door behind him, leaving all her secrets and pain as undisturbed as he had found them. He made his way down the staircase, through the hallway, out the front door, and sat on the porch swing facing the gravel driveway that would bring her back to him. Almost two hours later, long after dusk crawled away, Camilla's tires pounded against the rocks' surface, her lights creating a hazy halo around the man who awaited her on the porch swing, rocking back and forth with patience that belied the anger rising to his heated cheeks.

CHAPTER 19

"I waited up for you, Camilla." Carl's voice was like cold water washing over Camilla, its iciness stinging her flesh. She trembled and tucked her car keys into the center of her fist, the sharp edges of metal digging into her palm and making her wince.

"Why?" She stopped a few feet away from him, still standing on the dusted gravel, hoping the firm earth beneath her would give her the courage she needed to stand still, stand up straight, and face the man she loved and betrayed time and time again. She could only see his shadow from this vantage point, her below, him seated on the porch swing, not rocking back and forth, but just seated there, quietly taking her into his eyes, unfolding her layer by layer to see what she hid beneath. She tensed and made her body hold itself erect, unfoldable, unseeable. Hard. Impenetrable.

"I'm not a child. You don't need to wait up for me," she commanded when he didn't respond to her. She sensed fear rolling along the surface of her bones when he rose from the swing and took one step after another down the blue steps she painted so many years ago when everything between them had been new and simple. He stopped a few feet away from her, watching her with ashen eyes that seemed to take in every bit of her she didn't want him to see. He lifted his hand, and she flinched, taking a sudden step backwards.

"Are you afraid of me?" He asked, jerking his hand back as if spurned.

She shook her head, dark eyes brimming with tears. "I just can't bear for you to touch me."

She heard him suck in his breath as if she had just slapped him. "I don't mean it that way, Carl." Her voice was hushed, low. "I'm just not good enough for you anymore. I'm dirty. Soiled. I'm no good for you."

In the light, he could see the tears glide like a long trail of vines down her cheek, nestling into the outline of her lips, and disappearing into her mouth, which was open and taking in air with gulps, as if she were drowning.

"Let me decide how good you are for me, Camilla. I love you. There's nothing you can do to destroy that for me."

She opened her mouth to say something and then closed it again. Tilting her head, her hair falling off her shoulders like a cascade of water, she looked at him.

"You know."

"I know, what?"

"Don't play dumb with me, Carl," she snapped at him.

Carl sighed, his shoulders drooping, his arms loosening about his thighs, as if he were giving up. "About the men? Yes. I know. And I don't care."

"You don't care?" Her voice rose almost to a wailing echo that didn't sound human even to her. "Of course, you care. I can see it in your eyes. You're humiliated. You hate me."

"No," Carl's voice was like a soft breath against her cheek, a hand drawing soothing circles along the spine on her back. Camilla trembled with disbelief. He couldn't love her. Not now.

"Liar!" She seethed, her face so close to his now that he could smell the putrid remnants of beer on her breath. And something else, too, emanated from her skin. A stench that made his stomach turn. Sex. Beer and sex. He almost turned away from her, but not out of loathing. Out of hurt, pity even. But never out of loathing.

Carl moved towards her with slow precision, afraid she would panic and run away from him. "I know about the men, Camilla. And I don't care. You're in pain. We all do crazy things when we are in pain."

"Oh, yeah? What crazy things have you done, Carl?" He wanted to wipe the bitterness out of her voice as if it were a cluster of dust on his favorite table, with that kind of ease and deliberation, but he knew it wouldn't be easy. Nothing about Camilla was. Not anymore.

"Well, I just found your paintings that show me all the men you've had sex with, and I am not angry. I'm not leaving you. Some people would find that crazy." Carl paused and smiled at her, trying to lighten the load of his unearthing.

"I understand you, Camilla. You're in pain. You've suffered great losses and you're trying to hurt others the way that you hurt. Maybe even me. And I am hurt, but I understand, too. And I want to be there for you, to help you through this. You're not alone. You don't have to go through this alone, Camilla. I love you."

"Stop saying that." She shook her head at him, not wanting his words to soften her, to erase the hurt and loathing snarling and growling inside her like emaciated, feral dogs.

"I love you, Camilla." Carl said the words again, inching toward her with each uttered syllable until he could feel her muscles loosen at his nearness. He wrapped his arms around her and pulled her to him, an act intended to soothe and cocoon a wild, disbelieving animal.

Camilla pushed him away from her with a strength he had never encountered before, forcing him to stumble back a few steps.

"Well, I don't love you, Carl. I hate you. I hate you, you hear me?" Before she knew what was happening, Camilla stepped up to Carl and whipped her hand across his face, her fingers slicing into his cheek. She gasped at the red marks she left behind.

"Oh, God. I'm sorry. I'm so sorry." She choked back new tears, reaching out to touch his face with remorse written all over the lines on her forehead.

Carl swallowed back the sob he felt rolling into his mouth. He had never been struck before, and the sting of her fingers still vibrated on his skin. He took a deep breath and sat down on the blue steps, hoping she couldn't see the wetness in his eyes or the trembling in his hands. He moved over when she came near and sat beside him.

"I'm shit, Carl. I'm such shit. Don't you see that? I don't know what I'm doing anymore."

"I know," he murmured. "But I still love you, Camilla. I always will."

Camilla softened at his words this time, and she reached over to him, her arms winding around his shoulders, her fingers combing through the gray tendrils of his hair.

"Make love to me, Carl. Make me forget this aching feeling that won't go away. Take it away. Can you do that?" He nodded and turned toward her in the dark until his mouth found hers. She kissed him, climbed onto his lap, and began undoing the buttons on his shirt. They made love on the blue steps, as they had done many times before. But this time, their coupling was different. Hungry, impatient, desperate, as if they were trying to recapture a certain feeling that had been lost or expired. And later, when they lay on the steps in a naked heap, breathing heavily into each other's hair, they both felt empty and unsatisfied.

Without a word, they mechanically collected their clothing and made their way up the stairs, into their home, and enfolded themselves into the bed they shared, their backs to each other, eyes shut against the hollow echoes of secret misgivings they concealed from each other.

CHAPTER 20

Camilla awoke to the sound of chirping birds nested in the oak tree whose jagged boughs collided with the glass on her windowpane every morning, rain or shine, a tap-tapping vibrato intended to wake her from a deep sleep that insisted she stay in the dark, where it was quiet and still. She lay on her back, her limbs in a straight line, unmoving and numb. She wondered what it would be like to remain asleep. To sleep forever. Never to open one's eyes again. Never to love or hope, know pain or loss.

Turning her head toward Carl, she looked at the man she had made a home with, loved, unperturbed by the low snorts that escaped his nostrils. He was a stranger to her now. Just a man. A body lying beside her own, not touching, breathing to a different rhythm with which neither one could follow along. Even the melody was different. His song was still light, patient, quiet. Hers was a cacophony of minor chords, disjointed and untamed. They lay in the same bed, their shoulders inches apart, but they were separate entities. Polite strangers partitioned by the many barriers she had placed between them. Not deliberately, of course. But it had been her doing, and as much as she wanted to reach over to him right this instant and wipe the thick gray lock of hair from falling onto his closed lid, she pushed the desire out of her mind and clenched her fist to her chest so her fingers couldn't act against her will.

It had been days since the last time they had made love, if one could call it that. She smirked, almost aloud, and stifled the laughter that wanted to grip her entire body, mocking their estranged attempt at a coupling steeped in loathing and loss. Their bodies had met and meshed as one on the blue stairs that led to their porch and home, but neither of them had been present. As close as she had wanted to feel to Carl, as much as she hoped their coming together would make up for all the men she'd had sex with these past few months, Camilla understood that too much had passed between them. Perhaps too much pain had grown like mangled weeds refusing to be tamped down or controlled. It was out of their control.

Carl was thinking it, too, she knew. His pain hid in his bones, where he kept it so it wouldn't boil and fester, exposing its ugliness to the world. To her. He was a gentleman that way. Old-fashioned and stoic, the way men used to be, holding themselves up like tall, sturdy trees that only bent from decades of rain and storm winds pressing against their trunks, their roots embedded in layers of soil that stretched for miles beneath the surface. Carl was steady, resilient. For her. So she could lean on him and rest when it was all too much for her. Like now. Like this morning, waking up to life singing in her ears when all she wanted was to wrap her fingers around the damn bird's neck and wring the life out of it just to make it stop.

But Camilla was not made of the same ilk, the same strength. She was too weak to breathe on her own, too tired to move forward without a push from someone stronger. Her life was always off balance, waiting for a small earthquake to shake her awake and bring her back to reality. She thought Carl would be the one, the man who would push her, force her to stay, nurture independence and resilience in her character the way he nurtured these qualities in his plants, the tulips and roses and petunia bulbs he planted in the earth's soil, his fingers brown with dirt and patient with love. He watered them and watched them grow, and they returned to him each spring, as bright and colorful as they came to him the first year of their birth. He talked to them, reciting poetry from Byron and Keats, as if they were his children, their stems swaying with affection as they bowed to the warmth they found in the open palms of his hands, the soothing sound of his voice.

Camilla was no flower, and her body may have found some solace in his hands and nurturance for a while, but when it became too hard for her, she wilted. She was weak in places she believed did not exist. Glimpsing herself in the mirror, she only saw damage and surrender. Not the strong woman she wanted to be. She blamed her father for quietly abiding without fighting for her when she needed him most. When she was fifteen and had an affair with his best friend. When she had the abortion and he looked the other way. When her mother killed herself and he left Camilla all alone, pretending her mother had never existed, had not locked herself in the car, in their garage, with an empty bottle of sleeping pills beside her.

Camilla thought of her mother and was moved by the desire to paint her. Still in her sheer blue nightgown, she glided toward her studio, closed the door behind her, and sat in front of a white, naked canvas. She closed her eyes and tried to recapture her mother. Camilla barely remembered her and did not own any pictures with which to recollect the dark eyes smiling at her when she was little. Her father had taken all the pictures of his wife and tossed them into a box he shoved in the attic, along with all the other boxes containing her clothing, her shoes, and every other memory of the woman who betrayed him by taking her own life. After he died, Camilla looked for the box of pictures, wanting to scan over her mother's face, to find the actual frozen memories that remained in her thoughts of her mother and her at the park, unwrapping presents on Christmas morning, the times she helped Camilla blow out her birthday candles—all captured by the flash of a camera. But she never found them. She cleaned out the entire house, donated clothing and furniture until every room was as bare and clean as the canvas she was now staring at. He threw out every trace of his wife—Camilla's mother—long before he died. Without telling her. Without asking if she would want something belonging to the woman who had birthed her.

There was nothing tangible left of her mother. It's as if she had never lived, had never been the most precious part of Camilla's childhood. She did not understand why her mother had taken her own life, had abandoned her like that. Until now. Until the moment she tried to recapture the image of her mother that remained in her memory, her light brown hair, wavy and unruly, windswept like wildfire around her face. She was laughing, her hazel eyes changing color whenever the sun's rays struck them from a different angle. Camilla loved when they turned blue and she felt as if she was swimming in them, surrendering her limbs to lapping waves, calm and sonorous.

She had felt safe with her mother. That was always constant in her memories of her. Safety. Love. The recurring image of her mother picking her up and squeezing her against her chest, her lips covering every inch of her little face, and the words, "I love you so much," uttered into her ear, as if it were their secret. Camilla's mother had been affectionate with her, but not with her father. All her warmth and love were reserved only for little Camilla. They disappeared when Camilla's father came into the room. Laughter ceased. Smiles faltered. And coldness slipped into her mother's bones. Camilla remembered touching her mother's hand one day and shivering at how cold her fingers were in her grasp. She didn't remember her parents fighting or exchanging angry words. They were just quiet around each other. Distant.

Camilla shook her head and raised her paintbrush to the blank canvas, but nothing came to her. She wanted to paint a memory of her mother that flashed before her eyes. Her father had been at work, and Camilla was around four or five. She and her mother had a picnic with peanut butter and jelly sandwiches and apple juice in their backyard. Her mother brought the radio outside and flicked it on. The song "Pretty Woman" from Roy Orbison came on, and Camilla's mother got to her feet, bare and freshly manicured, her toenails painted bright red. Camilla giggled from her place on the blanket, watching her mother dance, her hair wild and free, her teeth straight and white as they bit her lower lip in concentration.

Camilla's mother pointed to her and curled her fingers, inviting her to join the reverie, but Camilla shook her head. She loved watching her mother, maybe because she was witnessing a rare occurrence. Her mother never danced, never expressed this much joy and freedom. Camilla recalled how powerful the image of her beautiful mother was, unfurled like a free flag left to soar in the wind without restrictions or inhibitions. And then her mother swayed toward her, picked her up from her armpits, and twirled her in circles, Camilla's arms and feet dangling in the air. She couldn't help but laugh as they both turned and turned on the grassy field, leaves cascading around them in their own wild dance as they detached from the tree branches above them and fell at their feet.

Camilla was surprised at the tears that slipped down her cheeks like honey, thick and sticky. She didn't stop them or wipe them away, and she couldn't understand why she was crying. Maybe because she never wept over her mother before. Not even when she found her in the garage, dead. Not even at the funeral. Camilla had not cried, but perhaps this was the loss she could never replace. The hole too big and wide inside of her that could never be filled, not by her father or Carl. And not through sex. She thought of all the times she tried to fill the emptiness in her chest her mother left behind. All the men she used, thinking the answer would be discovered in being loved by them. But it wasn't their love she needed all this time. It was her mother's love. The love given to her freely and willingly and then taken from her without warning. Without consideration for the little girl being left behind, left to the man her mother couldn't wait to get away from. If her mother couldn't stand to be with him, why would she surrender her own child to him? Camilla shook her head and the image of her mother's smile slowly departed, leaving behind only the struggle of trying to regain the look in her mother's eyes, the exact color of teal blue that enveloped Camilla in warmth and love and safety. But none of it would return to her, and she sat on her stool, hunched over the paints, the brush dangling from her loose fingertips until her mind was as blank of color and shape as the untouched canvas set before her.

After a while, Camilla left her studio, closed the door behind her, and made her way to the guest bathroom. She turned on the bath water and ran her fingers beneath the rush of it until it was hot enough to soothe her. Taking off all her clothes, she slipped her naked body into its warm depths, resting her head on the curved back of the porcelain tub that welcomed her. She placed a small washcloth behind her head to cushion her, soaped her legs, and then used Carl's razor to shave them. Camilla ran her fingers over them in case there were some patches she had missed, but confident her legs were free of hair and stubble from toes to her thighs, she placed them beneath the soapy water, encasing herself in a smooth blanket of heat and steam.

She eyed the razor for a few moments and then unscrewed the bottom, releasing the razor from its safe casing. She flicked the sliver of metal between her fingers, sharp and narrow in her grasp. And without thinking, without shrinking or flinching, she pressed the edge of the razor against her wrist and sliced her veins in half.

CHAPTER 21

Carl was awakened by the sun's incessant rays piercing through his closed lids, forcing them open. He pulled the pillow over his face to guard against the onslaught of the new day. He didn't want to wake up. He wanted to curl into a ball under the covers as he used to do when he was a little boy on Saturday mornings, when he didn't have to get out of bed for school or chess club or piano lessons. His mother, before she passed away, used to bring his breakfast to him, would tickle his face with a wild array of kisses, and leave the tray of eggs and bacon and orange juice on the table next to his bed.

"Eat it before it gets too cold," she warned him as she did every Saturday morning. It was their ritual. She let him sleep late, fed him, and left his room with a smile, knowing all too well that he wouldn't reach out of his blue and red plaid comforter until an hour later, when the eggs would be too cold and the juice would be tepid. But he ate it, shoving a forkful of food into his mouth, because he was famished and because his mother prepared it. For him. And he loved her. Even after she died and left him in the care of his father, a cold and withering man who never paid attention to his son or his wife. It only took him six months to replace her, to find another passive, doting woman to play house with him. But Carl never took to her. He had been ten at the time, and she and he circled around each other like anxious birds, afraid to linger or accidentally touch each other's wings.

When he was thirteen, his father put him in a boarding school in Upstate New York, and he grew up without a father or a mother but with the occasional annual visits home for Thanksgiving and Christmas, sitting around a table fraught with food Adele, the new wife, prepared for them, words pushed down and replaced with broccoli and chicken or turkey and mashed potatoes. It was so quiet. All the time.

As quiet as it was this morning, when he realized for the first time that Camilla was not lying in the bed beside him. He placed his hand in the area her body usually occupied, feeling only coldness there. Hollowness. He felt her absence every day since the last time they made love on the steps. They hadn't made love since. It's as if the spark that brought them together in the past had been squeezed in someone's fist, all traces erased from the memory of their bodies, so they did not know how to ignite it again. And so, it had been quiet between them. Quiet and eerily somber. They ate in silence, the only sounds daring to crash their wordlessness were the sounds of their teeth chewing food particles and their throats swallowing liquids they guided into their bodies like unseeing, unfeeling automatons. He went to work, she went to her studio, and at night, they went to bed, their backs to each other, a mutual numb "good night" breaking the awkward silence that stood like a stalwart oak between them neither had the means or strength to chop down.

Carl wiped the sleep out of his eyes with his forefingers, reached over to the table by his side of the bed, and grabbed his bifocals, pushing them onto the bridge of his nose. When his eyes adjusted to the light and the new day, he threw the covers off his weary body and raised himself until his feet touched the cool roasted almond hardwood floors of his bedroom. They were the same floors of his childhood, and this had been his childhood bedroom. He had occupied the spaces of this one room for decades, including the days of respite when he returned home from boarding school. His father left him this house when he died. Well, he actually left it to Adele, his bride, but she gave it to Carl, insisting it was his home and never truly belonged to her. She moved in with her sister in Florida until she died a few years later.

He took ownership of the home after graduating from college, but he kept it all the same. Had not changed a thing. The only additions to the home were the new books he ordered or purchased, layering his books alongside his father's collection of science textbooks, as he had been a Biology professor at the local community college until his death. Carl could not bring himself to get rid of his father's books, so he simply created a collection that reflected both men's tastes and professions. He loved books too much to get rid of them, and aside from the kitchen, which he cleaned before and after a meal, Carl only wiped off the dust from the books that adorned his wall-to-wall bookcases. Nothing else was worth anything of value to him in this home that had once belonged to his father.

There was no tangible trace of his mother in this home. Only memories of her humming a tune as she made dinner, or the hot steam that escaped the bathroom when she came out in a towel draped around her body after a long, hot shower. He could still recall the faint caress of the kisses she had planted on his cheeks and forehead and the tips of his fingers when she tucked him into bed at night, explaining to him that his father's daily slights, the way he dismissed him at dinner, or missed his baseball or chess club games had nothing to do with him.

"Your father is preoccupied," she would often remind him, her voice a soothing whisper against his hair. "He loves you. How could he not? You are a perfect little boy. A wonder. And I am so proud you are my child. He is proud of you, too. He may not say it, but he is."

"How do you know?" He asked her, tears skidding down his cheeks and landing at the corners of his mouth. "Does he tell you?" Carl wanted any affirmation of his father's love for him because he was never around. And when he was, he was silent, gruff, absent.

"He doesn't have to tell me. I know it. Just like I know he loves me, even though he doesn't say the words. He's just not a wordy man, but that doesn't mean the words aren't there. Trust me. I know."

But then she died, and there was no one to remind him that his father, or his mother, loved him anymore. He had been all alone until Camilla. Until she came into his life and saw him. Loved him, even though he was old and worn and abandoned on a shelf like an unwanted toy a child had grown out of but kept around as a reminder of his youth. She brought him back to life, and now? Well, now she too was gone. She was there, in his home, slept in his bed, sat opposite him during their meals together, but she was distant. It was like living with a ghost, and he didn't know what to do to make her live again. Breathe again. Smile again. Smile at him the way she used to. Every time she looked at him, it was like she was opening all the doors and windows, letting the stale air out and breathing new life into his home and his body. He missed her touch, the love she brought him and now took back, as if he no longer mattered. As if he was not even there.

Carl rubbed his eyes and set out to make coffee. It was Saturday morning, and it was raining outside, the sky gray and overcast as it bled tears of loneliness, chilling his already brittle bones. He trembled slightly and pulled the black sweater tighter across his chest. Making eggs and toast, he placed them on a tray, along with a mug of hot coffee for Camilla. He trudged up the stairs, tray teetering in his hands, and he placed it on the floor by her studio door.

"Camilla, I made eggs for you. And coffee." He knocked on the door, surprised when it gave way to the soft scrape of his knuckles. She often kept it locked, hiding in her painting, keeping her art and herself away from him.

"Camilla?" He pushed his head into the room, afraid that at any moment, a paint brush would come flinging at his head, something which only occurred once, when he first gifted the room to Camilla and walked in on her while she was painting. That was years ago. He learned not to interrupt the flow of her art, the absent-minded cadence of her brush strokes as they duplicated worlds and people living inside her thoughts. But nothing came crashing into his head. Camilla was not in her studio and the rest of the house was quiet.

He returned to their bedroom, hoping to see her in their bed, curled up and waiting for him to make love to her, the way they used to before everything between them became too knotted to unravel. But their bed was empty. He drew the curtains back as he looked for her car, but both cars were there, overcome by sheets of raindrops continuing to pour out of the sky with unrelenting ferocity.

Carl considered she might be taking a shower, but he didn't hear the water running from their joint bathroom. Then he noticed the door of the guest bathroom down the hall from their bedroom was closed, so he knocked on it. When no sounds came from within, he tried the doorknob. It was locked.

"Camilla," he called out to her, but still nothing. He knocked harder, called her name out louder. He put his ear on the door, hoping to capture some sort of movement indicating she was in there. But nothing stirred. It was still. And quiet. His heart pounded in his chest and a thick voice in his head told him to break down the door. He obeyed the voice, throwing his bony shoulders against the wooden structure again and again until it gave, and he was propelled into the small bathroom no one ever used.

And there she was, his Camilla. Lying in the tub, her dark hair like wet vines coiling around her face and throat, stuck to her skin. She looked peaceful, as if she had fallen asleep in the tub, and Carl almost smiled at the sight of her youthful face, her breasts peeking over the water's surface, her eyes closed against the darkness of the world she sought to escape.

His lips curled downward, and a sob escaped his mouth as his gray eyes took in the last image Camilla left of herself. Her right arm draped over the tub, her wrist cut, blood still leaking out of her and dripping onto the white tiles of the floor like rose petals falling off one by one, soft and fragile and perfectly red. Her left wrist, also sliced, lay on her chest, its blood flowing out of her and into the water. The contrast of red blood, of life pouring out of her body, against the pristine white backdrop of the tub and floor tiles was breathtaking. Wondrous. It was like looking into one of her paintings, and Carl wept with love and pain as they both coursed through his own veins when his gaze consumed the sight of her as if it were a rare and treasured gift he could never replace.

It reminded him so much of his mother, of the blood that had escaped her own body when he found her in this same tub so, so many years ago when he was only ten. He froze as he did back then, standing in her pool of blood, his toes soaked in red, still wearing his pajamas. He called for his dad and watched his father's face tremble with terror.

"Call 911, Carl. Now!" His father bellowed before picking up his wife's body from the bloodied tub and placing her on a bed of towels he laid out on the floor to cushion her loose limbs, drenched in blood and water. Carl ran downstairs and called 911 on their kitchen phone, but it was already too late. His mother was dead.

"Oh, Camilla," he cried into her hair and placed his fingers against her throat. He felt a pulse. It was weak, but it was there, and Carl sighed with relief. He unplugged the drain of the tub and watched as the bloodied water was swallowed and all but disappeared from his line of vision. He scrambled for the first-aid kit, cleaned the blood off her sliced wrists, and bandaged them as tight as he could, to keep the rest of her inside, where it belonged.

Scooping her up into his arms, he carried her to their bed, where he lay her down gently, dried the blood and wetness from her supple, cold skin, and then dressed her in her nicest nightgown made of light blue cotton. He piled two layers of blankets over her body, lay down beside her, and watched the pulse at her throat throb in and out, praying it would not stop. He fell asleep with his fingers on her chest, listening for the faint sounds of her heart beating in rhythm to his slow breathing.

CHAPTER 22

Chelsea pulled into the dusted driveway of Carl and Camilla's home. As she unfolded herself out of her car and made her way to the trunk to pull out a painting, her eyes filled with the exterior of the home that once resounded with Camilla's laughter rimming out of the opened windows, music vibrating against its foundation, the walls dancing to the rhythms Camilla chose for the occasion.

It was four in the afternoon, and there was no sound coming from the home. No laughter. No life, even. The house looked like it would crumble to pieces if she kicked just one of its beams, once creamy white, now brown and green with mold and neglect. The grass, overgrown with a yellow bed of weeds, consumed the red tulips that once rose to meet the porch structure, welcoming guests with vibrant colors that only faded when their season ended. Spider webs covered the porch, and many seasons' worth of dead leaves littered the area, having fallen from the oak trees towering over the roof, now bent with age and crooked boughs. The windows were dark with multiple layers of dust and grime stuck to them. Chelsea cleared one of them with her free hand to look inside, but the lights were out. There were no noises or movements coming from within the home, and she shuddered at the thought of what she would find once she made her way into the house.

She knocked on the main door a few times and then called out, glancing up at the second-floor windows in case Carl was looking to see who it was at the door. Chelsea considered leaving the painting on the porch, along with a rushed note that she would return the next day, but then thought twice about it. She imagined Carl or Camilla dead, or worse. Perhaps one had fallen down the stairs, unable to get back up. She couldn't leave without knowing if they were okay, so she knocked again, this time until her knuckles were raw and bruised from contact with the wooden structure standing between her and her friend.

Just as Chelsea reached into her purse to pull out her phone and call 911, she heard shuffling behind the door, followed by a loud click of the latch being unlocked, and saw the knob being turned. When the door widened, Chelsea gasped at the sight of Carl. He looked old and pale. Fragile, even. His appearance was that of a ninety-year-old man, his feet weak as they scraped along the floor, his fingers trembling violently as he brought his hands to his face, adjusting the glasses on his nose so he could peer closely at her.

"Carl. Hi. It's me, Chelsea." She forced a smile she hoped would not reveal her concern for his disheveled appearance. He was as neglected as his home was, worn and bent with fatigue and disuse. The gray eyes Camilla used to gush over during their talks and in her letters were glassy now, almost opaque. She wondered how long it was since he had seen an eye doctor. Or a regular physician as well. From the looks of him, it would appear to be years.

"Yes," his voice shook in rhythm to his fingers. "Chelsea." He said her name as if trying to recall who she was; there was no evidence of recognition in his gaze as he peered at her. "Was I expecting you?"

"No. I'm sorry. I came to collect my paintings from the gallery on Main Street, but I wanted to give you this. It's a painting of Camilla I made years ago. When she and I were living together. Long before she met you. I thought she'd like to have it." Chelsea pointed to the painting resting on the porch floor and leaning against her hips.

She caught him eyeing the painting but purposely kept the portrait hidden from him. She wanted to go inside the home, to see how they were living. She wouldn't leave without seeing Camilla this time. Even if it was for the last time, Chelsea wanted to make sure her friend was alright and was getting the help she needed. Looking at Carl, she wasn't sure he could take care of her, let alone himself.

"Come inside," Carl motioned for her to follow him as he pushed his feet along the floor's surface for forward mobility. Chelsea followed him inside the dark foyer, shutting the door behind her. A frigid chill ran along her fingers and up her arms, the way it did whenever one of her boys was hurt or showed her a bloodied knee or a scraped elbow. It was her body's warning to her, and she braced herself for what she would find inside the home she hadn't stepped a foot in for years at a time.

"Sit, sit." Carl pointed to the couch opposite his favorite chair and waited until she sat down before attempting to gather his loose bones and situate them into the center of the leather seat, covering the diagonal tear in the cushion. Chelsea shifted in her seat, trying not to pay attention to the laborious efforts of his movements as he used the feeble strength of his arms to balance himself into a seated position. He turned on the lights in the living room before he led her into it, so she could now observe the interior the dust and grime on the windows had barred her from seeing when she was waiting outside for him to open the door and let her in.

There were layers of dust on the bookcases, which told her he no longer read his treasured books. They seemed as untouched as the dirt and tattered fibers of the carpet her feet rested upon. Sliding her boot across the carpet out of curiosity, she saw a clearing of grime that revealed the rich red and brown fabric of its original design. Her eyes traveled upward to the cobwebs coiling around the lights and wires on the chandelier dangling loosely above her head. Chelsea inched closer to the corner of the couch just in case it fell on her head that very moment. Her movement startled a gray mouse, and it scampered from beneath the table to a small crack in the wall by the bookcase.

Chelsea swallowed the dry bile as it collected inside her mouth, but she was too afraid to ask Carl for water. The man who sat opposite her was no longer the confident man she had once known. Before her sat a thin and crumpled skeleton. He was all bones and sagging flesh, his cheekbones gaunt and hollow. She wondered when the last time he ate was and wanted to ask but was too afraid to offend him. She doubted he had any food in the house. His car was just as neglected as he was, and she was sure he had not left the house in a while considering the two flat tires and the muck on the windshields of both vehicles she had noticed upon her arrival.

"I brought you this," Chelsea turned the painting around so he could see the portrait she had painted a long time ago. "It's Camilla." She shifted forward in her seat and pushed it closer to him, noting his eyes were straining to capture the image of the girl on the canvas.

Carl raised his trembling hand in the painting's direction, as if to touch it, but lowered his fingers when he realized he couldn't reach. He leaned back in his chair as if surrendering and ran his gaze over the image of Camilla when she was young and vibrant, her mouth red and open with laughter.

"Camilla," he nodded with recognition. "She was so beautiful. She's still beautiful. She's upstairs, you know. Sleeping."

"I'd love to see her. It's been years, and the last time I was here, she was medicated. If you recall, I wasn't able to see her." Chelsea leaned the painting against the table between them and rose from the couch.

"I'll make you tea," he offered, but made no attempt to move. He was visibly winded from letting her in.

"Oh, no, Carl. Don't go to any trouble." Chelsea sat back down, afraid any sudden movement from him would kill him. She watched his chest heaving in and out as if an anvil had been placed upon it.

"Carl? Can I get you anything? Water? A doctor? You don't look too well."

"I'm fine. I look worse than I feel. I'm just old. Not as young as you and Camilla, that's for sure." His attempt at a laugh turned into a slow throaty cough full of phlegm that made his body convulse.

Chelsea jumped to her feet, swearing under her breath when another mouse scurried past her black boots, and she rushed into the kitchen to fetch him a glass of water. She ignored the pile of dishes in the sink caked with crumbs and a flurry of maggots crawling on the forks and knives abandoned on the counter, hardened sauce glued to the metallic surface of each, and went in search of a clean glass in the cupboard above the stove. When she located one good enough to wipe with her shirt, she filled it with water and took it back to the man still coughing up a storm.

"Thank you, my dear." Carl took the glass and brought it to his lips for a sip, but his hands were too shaky, and Chelsea had to guide the glass toward him, keeping it steady until he drank enough to soothe his throat.

"Carl. Where is Camilla?"

"I told you, dear. She's upstairs. Sleeping. She looks like an angel when she's asleep like that. You know," Carl straightened his spine and looked directly at her. "She always sleeps with a smile. She never believed me when I told her she slept smiling, but it's true. I love watching her sleep. So peaceful." He paused again, his lips parting into a grin as his memory unfolded into yet another endearing recollection of his wife.

Nodding, Chelsea took her seat opposite Carl again. She decided to wait him out. They didn't say a word, sitting comfortably in silence, and she watched him as he took in the young Camilla laughing at him from the surface of the painting she had brought over that evening. Soon after, he started nodding his head, and it only took a few more minutes for his chin to drop to his chest and remain there. He was asleep.

Chelsea moved slowly from the couch in the living room to the stairway in the foyer, looking over her shoulder at Carl's snoozing expressions as she took one step after another up the creaky steps leading to her friend. Although she hadn't been in the house for many years, she still remembered where the master bedroom was, and her feet pulled her in the direction of the back room from the top of the landing.

The door was closed, and when she turned the knob and pushed the door open, the full weight of rotting stench overtook her, forcing her to take a step back into the hallway. She remembered this smell from her childhood, whenever a mouse died in her father's garage, and she held her breath until he picked it up, sealed it in a garbage bag, and threw it in the trash on the side of their home. There were mice all over this house, so she didn't doubt if one or a few of them died and Carl could not see them or get rid of them. He couldn't seem to see past his nose, and she wondered how the hell he had taken care of himself and Camilla with no help. But Carl had never been one to ask for assistance. That much she knew about him. And neither was Camilla, for that matter.

"Camilla?" She whispered into the opening from the hallway, hoping not to wake Carl. She paused for a second and held her breath, releasing it again when she heard his slow snoring from below.

Chelsea lifted the collar of her sweater up to her chin and over her nose to ward off the stink that rushed to her nostrils as she treaded lightly into the bedroom. It was pitch black. She stopped short and held her breath to listen for Camilla's sounds. Any sounds, really. Camilla breathing, or snoring lightly, or coughing. But nothing came from the direction of the bed.

She traced her hand against the wall for the light switch, but then thought twice about flicking it. It would help her see into the room, but she didn't want to wake her friend or frighten her into having a heart attack. Chelsea felt for furniture instead. The reclining beige chair by the side of the bed. The dresser set back against the wall with a matching mirror Camilla had looked into the day she had married Carl, twirling to show her the way the hem of her skirt swished back and forth like a bell. There was also the solid earth-toned canopy bed in the center of the room that stretched out to the double bay window with sheer blue curtains overlooking Carl's garden, the large oak tree that doubled over the house no longer able to carry the weight of its existence, and the lake set all the way in the back of their property. She couldn't see any of that now, but she felt her way to the side of the bed she knew she would find Camilla.

She located a long protruding bump beneath the covers in the dark and slid her hands over the still shape until she was standing beside it.

"Camilla," she whispered, gently shaking what she believed to be shoulders, thin and bony beneath the fabric of her nightdress. "Honey, wake up. It's me, Chelsea. I've come to see you. To check on you, really. Are you awake?"

But there was nothing. Chelsea remembered there was a lamp next to the bed, so she moved her free hand to the direction of the small nightstand, her fingers blindly fishing for the lamp. When they located it, she moved her fingers up its spine until she felt the cord that would grant her light, and then she pulled it. It took a while for her eyes to adjust to the light, and when they were ready, she shifted them toward the shadowy figure lying beneath her other hand just in time to hear a wailing scream reach her ears.

Chelsea didn't realize the shrill sounds were coming from her own throat until her hand automatically clamped against her mouth to stifle them. She forced her eyes to take in the form lying on the bed before her, a carcass of bones and rotting flesh, dressed in a sheer blue nightgown. The only part of her friend she recognized was the brown hair cascading about her face, brushed out and carefully laid upon the pillow the skull belonging to it rested, the eye sockets hollow.

With heart pounding in her chest like a wild drum roll that would not cease, Chelsea ran from the room, down the stairs, and out the main door, leaving it wide open as she forced her heavy feet to follow the path leading to her car. Once inside, she pulled the door shut after her just in time to realize she had left her purse back in the house.

"Fuck, fuck, fuck," she yelled, slamming her fists against the wheel. It was only when she heard the jingle of her keys moving to the force of her pounding that she let out a throaty laugh. Her husband always teased her about leaving her keys in the ignition, and right at that moment, she was glad for her carelessness. It was the one habit she was thankful she hadn't been successful in breaking.

Turning the key in the ignition, she breathed a sigh of relief as her small Taurus began to grumble and then hum. The lights automatically swept over the gravel and she followed its path toward the house until her eyes met Carl's. He was standing by the open door, his hand in the air, his finger motioning for her to return. Back into the house.

As he moved toward her, gripping the porch railing and descending the teal blue steps one by one, Chelsea pulled the clutch to reverse and stepped on the gas, careening out of the driveway with a speed that paralleled the thrashing of her heart.

CHAPTER 23

Carl closed the door behind him as he reentered his home, turned off the lights in the foyer, and climbed back up the stairs Chelsea had fled down moments earlier in panic. He shook his head at the young woman, surprised she had run out so abruptly as to forget her purse. She didn't even say goodbye.

"Camilla, darling," he called out to his wife, still laying in the bed they had shared all these years. "What did you tell Chelsea to make her run out of here like that? She left her things behind. She'll need her wallet, I think. Perhaps she'll come back tomorrow for them."

Carl moved to Camilla's side of the bed and took in her features, small and radiant despite her age and the deterioration of her body. He was moved by her beauty, the way the light by the nightstand lamp struck her cheekbones and continued to radiate heat in his loins. She stirred desire in him even now, but he was too tired to pursue it tonight. Following Chelsea out of the house and maneuvering down the blue steps did him in. He placed the palm of his hand on his chest, willing his heart to slow down. He was breathless as he sat beside his wife, gazing down at her as she lay there, and he needed to catch his breath for a minute or two.

Clasping her cool hand in his, he leaned over and kissed her temple, then her lips and the long nape of her throat. He recalled all the times he had squeezed that same neck during their lovemaking, the way Camilla used to place his fingers around her throat and commanded him to "do it. Squeeze it. I like the feeling of blacking out during sex. It heightens my orgasm." He had never understood it, but the first time he had done it, squeezed the soft flesh with his fingers and watched her eyes go back inside her head, her red mouth open and gasping for air, it had excited him, too.

He chuckled thinking about it now, how much their lovemaking had been about giving up control and trusting one another. She had trusted him with her body, her sex, her desires. And he had trusted her with his own needs, which she had fulfilled with great enthusiasm and creativity. Images of their naked bodies rushed back into his thoughts, and he recalled the many occasions during which they had made love, in every room in this house, in their cars, beneath the tree by the lake, on a blanket laid out over the grass by the waterside.

"We've had a beautiful life together, Camilla. Rare in its beauty. You've made me so very happy," he whispered thickly in her ear, his lips tasting the fragile surface of the lobe he had spent many nights kissing and running his tongue over. She still smelled and tasted like the rose petals she used to pull from their stems and place all over her body, biting on the tip of one and placing in into his mouth with her own lips during their prolonged kiss, so that the petal tasted like the rose it belonged to and the inside of her mouth, remnants of coffee and sugar lingering on his tongue. He could taste her still, right this moment, and his fingers ran up and down the long, still shape of her body as it lay before him, stirring beneath his touch.

"Oh, Camilla," he sighed heavily, placing his head upon her chest, nuzzling his chapped lips over her breasts, now shrunken from sickness and old age. "I love you so much. Do you still love me, even though I'm so old, I can hardly make it up and down the stairs?"

She was wide awake now. He looked into her eyes, still dark and amorous as they gazed back at him, and he saw her answer there. He even caught the small upturn of her mouth as she attempted to grin at him.

"You flirt!" He chuckled, patting her thigh and pushing himself off the bed. "I have a gift for you. Chelsea brought it over."

He walked to the hallway and grabbed the painting of Camilla he had hauled up the stairs. Carrying it into the bedroom, he placed it on the dresser, against the dust-layered mirror that had not been cleaned in years.

"Is that centered?" He asked her, turning his head back in her direction to gauge her response. Her nod confirmed his decision to bring it to her, to share with her the portrait of a Camilla they had both known and loved. Young, vibrant, full of life and laughter that never ceased to inhabit her. He still saw these qualities in her, even though she hardly ever spoke or got out of bed. Ever since he had found her surrounded by her blood in the bathtub, her wrists slit in half, her insides trickling out of her like a steady stream of leaking water from a faulty faucet. He couldn't put the blood back into her already drained body, but he did his best to bandage her up, dressing her, brushing the gleaming strands of wet hair away from her face, and laying her in their bed. He had curled his body over hers and placed his head on the pillow they would share for the next ten years of their marriage.

Something was different now, though. Carl sensed it. His breathing was laborious, and his hand kept reaching to his chest to ease the knots collecting beneath his ribcage. He lay down beside Camilla for a few moments and hoped for some rest.

Pushing his head against the yellowed pillow until he was comfortable, Carl faced his wife, picked up her hand, thin and cold to the touch, and laid it on his chest, locking it in place with his left hand. He moved closer to her side of the bed and positioned his free hand on her chest. A surge of fire passed through his body and another spasm gripped his chest as if a clenched fist flexed inside of him. He surrendered to the blackness that overtook him, shutting his eyes against the flashing red and blue lights outside his window and Camilla, staring back at him, the playful look in her eyes beckoning him to join her.

THE END

ACKNOWLEDGMENTS

My gratitude primarily goes to Joe and our children, Joseph and Marina, for making my writing part of our family discussions and for giving me the time and space needed to be a writer. Without their participation and support, this book would not have been written. It is for them that I write and endeavor to fulfill my dreams, so they can learn to make their own dreams a reality.

Thank you to Reagan Rothe and the staff of Black Rose Writing for offering me a generous contract in publishing my book and making the process so easy and flawless.

Many thanks to my Women's Fiction Writers Association (WFWA)peers, and special gratitude to Michele Montgomery for organizing and sustaining daily writing Zooms during the pandemic. You provided a safe and trusting space for all of us to create and revise as well as console and advise each other. I've never written as much as I have since joining this organization and this virtual writing space. Thank you to all my WFWA sisters for showing up, reading, and supporting this invaluable work we do out of love.

ABOUT THE AUTHOR

Author of the award-winning debut novel, *Dear Jane*, Marina DelVecchio is a college professor and writer who focuses her work on the internal and external struggles of women. Her writing can be found online and in print. Born in Greece and raised in New York, she currently lives with her family in North Carolina.

NOTE FROM THE AUTHOR

Word-of-mouth is crucial for any author to succeed. If you enjoyed *The Professor's Wife*, please leave a review online—anywhere you are able. Even if it's just a sentence or two. It would make all the difference and would be very much appreciated.

Thanks!
Marina DelVecchio

We hope you enjoyed reading this title from:

BLACK ROSE
writing™

www.blackrosewriting.com

Subscribe to our mailing list – *The Rosevine* – and receive
FREE books, daily deals, and stay current with news about
upcoming releases and our hottest authors.
Scan the QR code below to sign up.

Already a subscriber? Please accept a sincere thank you for
being a fan of Black Rose Writing authors.

View other Black Rose Writing titles at
www.blackrosewriting.com/books and use promo code
PRINT to receive a **20% discount** when purchasing.